the other side of death

the other

side of death

Judith Van Gieson

UNIVERSITY OF NEW MEXICO
ALBUQUERQUE

©1991 by Judith Van Gieson
University of New Mexico Press paperback edition 2003
Published by arrangement with the author. All rights reserved.
Originally published by HarperCollins Publishers, 1991,
ISBN 0-06-016581-2 (CLOTH)

Library of Congress Cataloging-In-Publication Data

Van Gieson, Judith
The other side of death / Judith Van Gieson
p. cm.
ISBN 0-8263-3207-2 (alk. paper)
1. Hamel, Neil (Fictitious character)—Fiction.
2. Pueblo Indians—Antiquities—Fiction.
3. Albuquerque (N.M.)—Fiction.
4. Women lawyers—Fiction.
I. Title.

PS3572. A42224 O85 2003
813'.54—dc21
2002044405

For my New Mexican friends

Other Judith Van Gieson books in the Neil Hamel Mystery Series

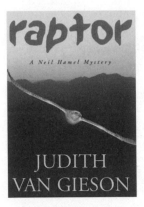

Raptor
ISBN 0-8263-2974-8

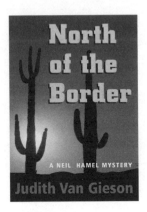

North of the Border
ISBN 0-8263-2886-5

 University of **New Mexico** Press
1-800-249-7737

Other Judith Van Gieson books in the Claire Reynier
Mystery Series

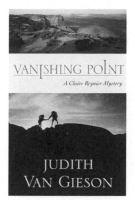

The Stolen Blue
ISBN 0-8263-2233-6

Vanishing Point
ISBN 0-8263-2383-9

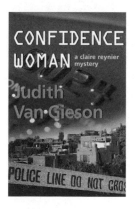

Confidence Woman
ISBN 0-8263-2888-1

Land of Burning Heat
ISBN 0-8263-3172-6

Visit our website and order online at
www.unmpress.com

1

Spring moves north about as fast as a person on foot would—fifteen to twenty miles a day. It crosses the border at El Paso and enters New Mexico at Fort Bliss. Like a wetback following the twists of the Rio Grande, it wanders through Las Cruces and Radium Springs, brings chili back to Hatch. A few more days and it has entered Truth or Consequences and Elephant Butte. The whooping cranes leave Bosque del Apache, relief comes to Socorro. Los Lunas, Peralta, and Bosque Farms take a weekend, maybe. By mid-March the season gets to those of us who live in the Duke City, Albuquerque. On 12th Street, fruit trees blossom in ice cream colors. The pansies return with purple vigor to the concrete bins at Civic Plaza. The Lobos are eliminated from NCAA competition. The hookers on East Central hike up their skirts. The cholos in Roosevelt Park rip the sleeves off their black T-shirts, exposing the purple bruises of tattoos. The boys at UNM take their T-shirts off, exposing peach fuzz. Women at Pyramid Holiday Inn pick up their pillows, pay three hundred dollars and go within for a Shirley MacLaine seminar. Guys in Crossroads Park take their camouflage jackets off and lay their bedrolls down for free, burned-out Vietnam vets in spirit or in fact. Tumbleweeds dance across Nine Mile Hill and get caught in a sign that says DANGEROUS CROSSWINDS. Between the snake garden and the mobile home community the Motel Nine offers a room for $12.95 with a video of *Wild Thang*.

At my place in La Vista Luxury Apartment Complex, the yellow shag carpet needed mowing; the Kid's hair was getting a trim. His hair is thick, black and wound tight and the way to cut it is to pull out a curl and lop off an inch. The hair bounces back, the Kid's head looks a little narrower, the floor gets littered with curls.

He sat, skinny and bare chested, in front of my bedroom mirror, and I took a hand mirror and moved it around behind him so he could see the effect of the trim. "Looks good, Chiquita," he said. I vacuumed up the curls and helped him out of his jeans, then we got into bed.

The afternoon is the very best time: the window open to the sound of kids playing in the arroyo, motorcycles revving in the parking lot, boom box music but not too close, the polyester drapes not quite closed and sunlight playing across the wall and the Kid's skin. Warm enough to be nice and sweaty, but not so hot as to stick together. And in the breeze the reckless, restless wanderer—spring.

"Oh, my God," I said in a way I hadn't all winter.

"*Chiquita mia,*" said the Kid.

The Trojans that had defined our relationship and been our protection for the last six months had remained in the bedside table. I promised them that would never ever happen again.

*   *   *

That was Saturday afternoon. In the evening the Kid played the accordion at El Lobo Bar in the barrio. He works as a mechanic during the day, an accordion player at night—the money goes back home to Mexico. I was on my way to my friends Tim and Jamie Malone's annual Saint Patrick's Day party in Dolendo. They were still calling it their annual party, but they hadn't held it in years and I hadn't seen them in those years either. They were friends from the Old Mexico days in San Miguel de Allende, where I'd spent the year between college and law school deciding what to do next. In some places the sixties spirit lasted well into the seventies; that was one. It was a small town full of gringos given to excess. Blake said that road leads to the palace of wisdom, but sometimes it leads only to further excess. The San Miguel crowd hung out in the plaza together, drank together, took drugs together, slept together. When the need to make a living intervened, a number of us ended up in New Mexico, the closest thing to Old Mexico, but as the years went by and we went our separate ways, I'd lost touch. I had settled in Albuquerque and was making a living (more or less) as a lawyer. The others lived around the City Different—Santa Fe—poets, artists, waitresses, Roto-Rooter men. It's a magnet for seekers of all kinds and some people will do whatever it takes to live there. The occasion for renewing the tradition was the end of it—the Malones were moving to Ohio.

"Ohio?" I asked when Tim called to tell me.

"I know, I know. I'll tell you all about it if you come to the party."   .

"You'll have to do some fast talking to explain Ohio to a New Mexican."

"It's what I do best," he replied.

Before sending the Kid off to work, I fixed him a snack of chips and salsa, gave him a beer and a kiss.

"What time you be home, Chiquita?" he asked on his way out the door.

"Well . . ." The last Saint Patrick's Day party I went to was still alive when I left at three A.M., but the times had changed and Tim had probably changed with them if he was moving to Ohio. "Not too late," I said.

The Kid yawned and stretched. "Maybe I go home to-night after I play the accordion."

"See you tomorrow?" It would, after all, be the second day of spring.

"*Claro,*" he said. "*Mañana.*"

Dolendo, like most towns in northern New Mexico, has a beautiful old church at its center made out of mud and water, sweat and straw. Adobes of God, they call them. Dolendo also has more than its share of artists, poets, seekers and seers. Twenty miles of wide open spaces from Santa Fe, it's a spiritual suburb. From Albuquerque it's sixty-five to eighty miles north depending on which way you go, but any way you go is spectacular. In fact, once you get away from the buildings erected by the conquistadors of the last four centuries the whole state of New Mexico is spectacular.

Spring was four or five days away from Dolendo—more maybe, factoring in an increase in altitude. The cottonwoods, long-limbed dancers on the wind, hadn't leafed yet; their black shadows stretched across riverbeds and lawns. The Malones' house sat on a rise at the edge of town with a cemetery behind it and an ocean of piñon in front. As far as you could see to the south there was nothing but green piñon bushes and blue sky and beyond that—more. I took a picture of the house from the cemetery once; both the middle distance and the far came out like deep-water, long-distance blue. Tim sat in his window day after day and wrote poetry but he should have built a wall around him,

4

because in front of a view like that it was hard to believe anything you did or ever could do mattered.

Tim and Jamie got married when they were teenagers, and had now owned this house—their first and only—for close to twenty years. It's what is called a puddled adobe, poured mud—the way they used to build houses in New Mexico. The walls are three feet thick and keep the heat in in winter, out in summer. In a puddled adobe house there are no right angles or straight lines. All soft curves and rounded corners, it seems to be rising out of the ground at the same time that it sinks back in.

I made a right at the church, a left, another right and turned up their bone-rattling dirt driveway, which was corrugated with dried mud. Ten to fifteen cars were parked among the ruts and Tim happened to be outside when I arrived looking for Foxy Lady, his dog. He spotted my orange Rabbit and ambled over.

"Still driving the shitmobile," he said.

"Pleasure to see you, too, Tim."

"Your car's a junker, darlin', but you know I love you and I always will." He opened his arms wide and I walked in. "Pretty as ever," he whispered in my ear.

"Not *that* pretty," I replied. We separated and I took a good look at him. "You're not looking so bad yourself." His curly brown hair was turning gray, but his belly had stopped hanging over his belt buckle and his cheeks were less ruddy than they'd once been. His eyes still had the startled expression of a baby taking its first good look at the world, but they were clear. On the wagon again. He was an outrageous drunk, not much different sober, an Irishman, and that was compounded by having grown up in Mexico where his father worked. I told him once that I thought the Irish were Britain's Mexicans. "You've got a point, darlin'," he said. "Only the Brits swallowed up our culture, language and all, and that will never happen to the

Mexicans. They're the ones who will be doin' the swallowin'."

He took my arm. "No more drinking, no more smoking. I'm livin' the sober life now. Come with me, take a walk on the tame side."

"Where?"

"The cemetery. Jamie wants the dog in and she's up there digging up bones—not the dead's, ones she buried. Foxy?" he yelled. The dog didn't answer.

I have a weakness for old cemeteries, and Dolendo's is one of the best. It's filled with wooden crosses and crooked tombstones telling stories of the prematurely stricken and the miraculous survivors. Take the Ortiz family. In the 1800s Margarita lived to be 25, Pablito 7 and Josecito 5, but Jose made it to 1929 and 101. The bad news is that sooner or later you're going to end up just like them, but it helps to know so many have gone first. A couple of Foxy Lady's buddies who had been headed toward the cemetery hadn't made it. We found their bodies, decaying lumps on the ground, noses pointed toward the gate. "Even the dogs are dying to get in," said Tim.

"Did you bring me up here just to say *that?*" I asked.

"You know me too well, darlin'," he replied.

"Not that well," I said, because when it comes to somebody else's husband I've learned there's always a far side to them you'll never know.

There was a flurry of dirt behind a tombstone. "Foxy," Tim yelled. "Get your ass on over here." She peered out at us, a red mutt with a long tail whose nose was covered with dirt. "Damn bitch," muttered Tim. "Come over here or I'll sic the hawk on you." Foxy gave her tail a shake and went on digging.

"The hawk? Aren't you promising more than you can deliver?"

"Not necessarily. The neighbors lost their cat to a hawk.

When they moved here from California, the cat, an expensive Persian, refused to go outside and it had always liked being out before. After a couple of years in the place, they finally coaxed it through the door. It climbed the wall, and a hawk swooped down, picked it up in its talons and carried it away. When it runs out of cats, Foxy, you'll be next." He went behind the tombstone and pulled Foxy out, and we began walking back to the house.

"Is that why you're leaving Dolendo, afraid of the hawk?"

"No, we're leaving because my messenger-service business went under and Jamie was offered a job in Columbus teaching pottery."

"How do you feel about it?"

"I haven't made my mind up yet, but I'll tell you one thing." He waved his arm around the cemetery then swung it toward the long view. It was a place that raised the big questions. "I'm tired of living in the middle of a fucking religious experience. We've got the house rented for a year. Maybe we'll come back, maybe we won't. Wait 'til you see what Jamie's done to the place."

"Put in some more windows?" I'd been at the Malones' one New Year's Day bored stupid by the groans and grunts of television football when Jamie decided she wanted a new window in the bathroom. She picked up a sledgehammer and smashed a hole in the wall. You can do that with adobe.

Tim laughed. "A whole lot more than that." He pushed Foxy Lady toward his front door and just before we got there he said, "Lonnie's here; she wants to see you."

Jamie was waiting for us behind the heavy wooden door. "Stay in the house, Foxy," she said. The dog grinned, wagged her tail and disappeared inside.

You wonder sometimes what keeps two people together. A week of it could be compared to a short flight on a commuter line; twenty years would be a voyage to Neptune to me. When I see Jamie, though, it makes some sense. She's a tall woman, Tim's size. They used to wear each other's clothes, maybe they still did. She has large brown eyes and wears her hair hanging down her back, the kind of hair that falls into place and ends in a straight line. She's a woman who pays attention to the small things and in the middle of a party worries about her dog, a woman who keeps her head when everybody else is losing theirs, a woman who would hold her marriage together no matter what the cost, but maybe for her the cost wasn't that great. It seemed to be her nature to be a partner and a rock.

"Good to see you, Neil." She gave me a hug.

"You, too, Jamie."

"What do you think of the house?"

It used to be one large room and when the two of them needed psychic space, they imagined more. "I'm going into the den now," Tim would say when he wanted to write. "Okay," Jamie'd reply and go on ignoring him. From what I could see over and around the guests, they'd added some rooms, more windows, beams (called vigas around here) in the ceiling, a kiva fireplace, smooth pastel walls, Mexican tiles in the kitchen, a polished wood floor. Dolendo dirt-floor poverty had turned into Santa Fe style. Jamie was in her stocking feet, probably to protect the new floors. She eyed my running shoes suspiciously but she didn't make me take them off. "It's a change, all right," I said. "Did you do all this yourself?"

"Not exactly, I contracted it out, but that was a job, too." Expensive, besides. I wondered, briefly, how the Malones, one potter and one failed messenger-service operator and poet, had paid for it. They'd been broke as long as I'd known them.

"Now that you've made it so beautiful, aren't you sad to leave?"

"No," said Jamie.

Tim had wandered off among his Hispanic neighbors. Some of them were playing down-home music—a fiddle, a guitar, an accordion—that blended well with the sound of Hispanics speaking English. Native Spanish speakers have a way of singing the English language and rounding off its corners, but Anglos put angles in Spanish where they've never been.

Jamie and I squeezed into the kitchen, my mind on some ice for the Cuervo Gold I'd brought. A table was covered on one side with bowls of posole, chile, chips, beans, a pot of chile con queso, on the other with bean sprout salad, tabouli, sesame noodles, whole-grain bread. A New Age woman was leaning against the dishwasher talking, a tall woman with a silver voice wearing a silver dress. She had a thick black mane parted down the middle with silver streaks that framed her face. Her eyes were turquoise blue. Her dress was made of some kind of thin, pale fabric, with a zigzag ankle-length hem, embroidered everywhere with lightning bolts of silver sequins, a dress you'd notice in a crowd. It was what they call wearable art in Santa Fe and only Hollywood actresses, rich Texans and expensive psychics could afford it, Santa Fe being one place in America where psychics make more money than lawyers. A psychic or an actress, I figured when the woman spoke, because a Texan's voice has more oil in it than silver.

"The center of Uranus is ice cold," I heard her say.

"That's Ci," said Jamie, "the psychic. You have to have at least one at a party around here."

The only way to get to the refrigerator was to press between C (or was it Sea?) and her audience. "Excuse us." Jamie interrupted the monologue and introduced me since I was six inches away from the woman's nose. "Ci, this is Neil Hamel."

"Neil?" she asked.

"N-e-i-l," I spelled it out.

"The man's name. I like it. Short, simple, expressive of the Martian nature, the masculine, take-charge side. Most women have chosen names more aligned with Venus, but a name like Neil . . . now that makes a statement. What do you do?"

"I'm a lawyer."

"Of course." She smiled.

"And I didn't choose my name; I inherited it from my uncle, Neil Hamel, who was with the Tenth Mountain Division in World War II," I said.

"Named after the warrior uncle. Mars *is* the god of war, you know. I see something Martian about you, a very strong element or a weak one masquerading as strong. Mars does that sometimes. In the larger scheme we all choose our own names just as we all choose our parents and the moment when we incarnate."

I was about to choose a nice, cold tequila if I could find some ice. "Excuse me, Sea. . . ." I began inching past.

"Ci is short for Cielo. It means . . ."

"I know what *cielo* means."

"Sky. In Spanish."

"Bedspread, too," I said. Jamie had gotten waylaid by a guest, and I was on my own when it came to finding the ice. There wasn't any. No ice bucket, and the trays in the freezer had been emptied before I got there. A large pot was brewing coffee. Some bottles of lemon-lime seltzer, raspberry ginger ale and white zinfandel in a clear bottle littered the Mexican-tiled counter—soda or disguised as same. I remembered when it used to be white chablis in a green bottle or clear liquor in a clear bottle. The only colored drinks were the ones the Mexicans drank out of plastic bags. I poured some Cuervo Gold into a paper cup. A guy with blond Rastafarian ringlets and an embroidered Guatemalan shirt was helping himself to a coffee.

"Decaf," he said, filling a Styrofoam cup.

"Tequila," said I.

"You still drinking that stuff?" He shook his head.

"You still wearing those shirts?" I asked. Guatemalan shirts had disappeared a decade ago from most places, but in pockets of northern New Mexico they still dressed like hippies, even though they drank like yuppies.

"You're not from around here, are you?" the guy asked.

"Albuquerque," I said.

"Albuquerque, jeez." He shook his blond Rasta curls. "I've never understood how anyone can live *there.*"

I was rescued from this dead-end conversation by an arm around my shoulder, a face full of blond hair.

"Neil."

"Lonnie."

"Good to see you again."

"How have you been?"

"Great."

"You look wonderful."

"So do you."

Actually, Lonnie looked worn out, but she always had, it was part of her appeal. Her hair was thin and frizzy and she bleached it almost beyond repair. She had a soft, voluptuous body that was always on the verge of turning to fat, but hadn't yet. Fair-haired and delicate when she was on, frowzy when she wasn't, she was often pretty, always vulnerable, the kind of woman men love, leave and love all over again.

"The steps you take in this life set up the karma for the next one," Ci said . . . loudly.

"Is that what you call psychic babble?" I asked Lonnie, leading her to the far side of the kitchen where the kind of stove with burners that are part of the counter filled the spot where once an ancient wood stove had been.

Lonnie laughed. "She babbles for bucks. Ci's hot stuff

11

right now. The psychic of the moment. What do you think of her hair?"

"On her I like it."

"Sometimes I think I'll let my hair go gray when the time comes," Lonnie sighed. "It doesn't look so bad if you've got a young face." Lonnie had the face of a young woman older than her years or an older woman who still looks young. Somehow the fine age lines didn't fit, which happens sometimes to fair and thin-skinned women. "Ci washes her hair in Perrier."

"Give me a break."

"It gives it body, she says."

"What's her act?"

"She used to be an astrologer. Now she takes people into their next incarnation, forward life progression, she calls it. It's an amazing experience, Neil. You ought to try it sometime."

"I've got enough problems in this life, thanks."

"What you do in this one determines what will happen in the next, Ci says."

"A futuristic Shirley MacLaine. Does that mean it's okay to have an affair with a married man in this lifetime if you plan to suffer for it in the next?"

"Shirley MacLaine stiffed me. Did I ever tell you that? When I was a bartender at La Posada. I waited on her all night and she took off without leaving me one thin dime."

That had been Lonnie's life, rotten jobs, no tips, and bad men, too. "What are you doing these days to support yourself?" I asked. In the time I'd known her she'd been a bartender, a landscape artist, a real estate agent, a messenger for Tim's Helio Courier Messenger Service—a typical career in Santa Fe, where there are fifty applicants for every crummy job. Most people who follow that path are trying to be artists or artisans. As far as I knew, Lonnie had just been following a man.

"I'm the manager of the Sangre de Cristo Health Club."

"The Blood of Christ Health Club?"

"That's it." She poured herself some white zinfandel.

The top buttons of Lonnie's shirt had come undone. Pinned to the shirt was a "no" button with a red line drawn across the word UGLY. I'd seen Lonnie look better, but even at her worst, she wasn't ugly.

"Why the button?" I asked.

"I'm on the Committee to Stop the Ugly Building," she replied. "First Associates wants to put up a truly hideous office building on Paloma. It'll be the tallest, largest, ugliest building in Santa Fe. It will fill the whole block, hide the view, dominate and ruin the entire downtown area." A cause. Lonnie had been involved in them as long as I'd known her. She'd been unable to ban the bomb, save the whales, the dolphins or the baby seals either. The Vietnam war ended finally, however, I'd give her some credit for that.

"Are there any tenants lined up for this building?" I asked.

"The Zia Bank has the ground floor and the Santa Fe branch of your old law firm, Lovell, Cruse, Vigil and Roberts, has the two top floors."

They'd be the first to arrive on the doorstep of something ugly.

"You could help us by talking to them, Neil." The wine in her paper cup masqueraded as pink soda and that's how Lonnie was drinking it. She poured herself some more.

"Believe me. I'm the last person Lovell, Cruse, Vigil and Roberts would listen to. You did say the architect for this Ugly Building is First Associates?"

"Rick himself. Doesn't it make you sick?"

Rick First was an architect Lonnie had been involved with off and on ever since I'd known them both in San Miguel de Allende. They'd been married for a few years

13

but that didn't bring them together. Then they got divorced and that hadn't torn them apart.

"What does Rick think about this?" I pointed to the UGLY button.

"He's pissed. It's over between us, Neil." She spun the wine around in her cup.

"I've heard that before."

"No. This time it's really over. He has someone else."

I'd heard that before, too.

"This one's a real estate developer from Texas with megabucks who's helping to finance the Ugly Building. Giving Rick a chance to make a name for himself. Can you believe it? Rick with a shark-faced real estate developer? Christ. Her name is Marci Coyle, Marci with an *i*—like I said, she's from Texas." Lonnie's lips puckered when she mouthed the name as if her zinfandel had been made with sour cherries. "Rick's gotten as greedy as everyone else these days."

Always one to keep up with the times. In the extended sixties when I knew him—better than I should have, I'll admit it—Rick First was a dope-smoking hippie, more interested in drugs and sex than money or architecture. I could see the appeal to a guy like that of a rich and powerful woman. I could also see the appeal of a Lonnie who'd always be down there for him to fall on. A Marci Coyle, on the other hand, might expect a return on her investment.

"Darlins." Tim was filling up at the decaf machine.

"Timito." I called him by his San Miguel nickname.

"Timber," said Lonnie, leaning sideways until she fell on him.

"Neil, come on over here." Tim squeezed me against his other side. "Sandwiched between two of my favorite women, right where I want to be."

"If we're the white bread, then what does that make you?" I asked.

14

"The meat. I'll be the meat in your sandwich any day."

"Baloney," said Lonnie. "Baloney, Maloney."

"Lonnie, Lonnie, Lonnie." Tim pulled her tight. "I'm the man your mother warned you about."

"Don't you wish," she said.

Jamie wasn't visible, but if she had been, she probably would have ignored us. No one is as flirtatious as a safely married man. I'd always thought Tim carried on like this because he was anchored and married. Lonnie, who was neither, leaned on him hard. It was a risk for Tim to be on the wagon at a party, but risk taking is the luxury of people with something to lose. The steps Lonnie took that might seem risky to some had always looked to me like a grab at security.

I was ready for another Cuervo Gold, so I peeled Tim's arm off and searched the kitchen counter, pushing aside empty, nonreturnable soda bottles, seltzer bottles and Styrofoam cups with the dregs of decaf in the bottom. "God damn it," I said, "somebody took my bottle."

"Now darlin', why would anybody do that," Tim asked, "when nobody drinks spirits anymore in Dolendo?"

"You mean they don't drink their own."

"Have a decaf," said Tim.

"I never drink that stuff. How can you be sure it's real? At least when you drink tequila you know you'll be asleep at three in the morning."

"*I* know it's decaf," said Tim. "I made it myself."

"You know, Tim, what I used to enjoy about your parties was that there was always someone there behaving worse than yourself." I lit a cigarette. "Now everybody's gotten the holies."

"I'm not *that* holy," said Tim. "How about you?" He gave Lonnie a tighter squeeze.

"Me neither," she replied.

2

A good party has a rhythm: ice clinks in glasses, someone keeps turning the volume on the music up, conversations get louder and dumber, flirtations flare, smoke thickens. At this party someone kept turning the volume down, the band went home early, no one smoked but me. Styrofoam cups don't clink. By ten forty-five the house had emptied into islands of halfhearted partyers. I got tired of making sober conversation, had a cup of decaf for the road and said good-bye: to Foxy Lady, who hit me up for a cracker; to Jamie, whom I hoped to see again before she left; to Tim; and to Lonnie, who was leaning against the wall with one more button undone on her shirt.

The party's not over till the drunk lady leaves, and it's not spring till it's spring in New Mexico. It had been close to seventy degrees when I left Albuquerque a few hours before. While we'd partied soberly, winter returned to Dolendo. It has a way of hanging on in the higher elevations. "Shit," I said, dodging snowflakes as I ran to my

Rabbit, expecting to turn the fan to six and the heat all the way to the right and shiver until the car warmed up. When I turned the key in the ignition the radio came on, but the engine didn't. The radio was tuned to KJOY—killjoy, I thought as the starter made a cranking noise, whirred and then shut up. I turned the radio off, tried again, heard the rattle of money, then nothing but the March wind and my chattering teeth. "You're a pain in the ass," I said to the Rabbit. One of nature's laws is that when your life is falling apart, your car won't run. But my life wasn't so bad; this breakdown was out of sync. I abandoned the car and ran back to the house. When I pulled open the heavy wooden door snowflakes swirled around me like I was the ghost of winter past.

"Look what the wind blew in," Tim said.

"Winter all over again," I replied.

"Darlin', you know we always have at least two winters here before we get spring."

"My car won't start."

"Maybe the battery's dead. I've got jumper cables if you need 'em."

"It's not the battery—the radio still works. It's something worse."

"Neil, I think it's time for a professional woman like yourself to get a new car or a new mechanic."

"I'm happy with my mechanic, thanks."

"A new car then."

"I don't want a new car." Ugly and unreliable as *el conejo*, the orange Rabbit, was, it was paid for. My checkbook had no place in it for car payments, none for repairs either.

"I don't know anybody we can call at this hour. What do you want to do?" asked Tim. A lot of men would have gone out there and insisted on trying to start the car themselves, but I'd never known Tim to waste time being macho about the small things.

"You got me." I couldn't ask the Kid to drive all the way up here in a snowstorm, besides it was a quarter to eleven and he'd only be on his first set at El Lobo.

"Come into Santa Fe with me, spend the night and worry about your car in the morning," Lonnie said, standing upright and buttoning her shirt. "I've got a sleeping bag and a blanket in the car if we run into any trouble."

"It's not snowing *that* bad," I said. She had a point about Santa Fe. I'd rather be in town where at least you could rent a car than be stuck out here. Besides Lonnie looked like she could use some help with her driving.

"Okay," I said, "*Andale.* Let's go." I moved toward the door, but Lonnie was into long and sappy good-byes with lots of hugs and kisses and see you soons. She lingered, lingered and lingered some more. When I couldn't stand it any longer, I opened the door and let some winter blow in.

"It's time to go, Lonnie," said Jamie, pushing her out.

Lonnie hadn't dressed for winter either, and we ran to her car, a yellow Nissan. She was wearing high-heeled boots and she tripped in a rut and fell. I helped her back up. "Give me the car keys, Lonnie," I said.

"I can drive, Neil."

"I can drive better."

"I'm a good driver."

"Maybe, but I only had one short tequila hours ago, and you've had a whole bunch of white zinfandels."

"Not that much. I can drive."

"Lonnie, give me the keys." We stood at the door to the Nissan shivering in the wind.

"Oh, all right, if you're going to be like that about it." She was pissed but she gave up and got in the passenger side. I shook my head and brushed the snow off before I got in the car, but she didn't bother. For a few minutes before it melted the snow lingered on her hair and turned it prematurely white.

The Nissan started right up. Lonnie pulled the sleeping bag out of the backseat, wrapped it around her and sulked in her corner. I backed out of the driveway, turned left and met three snarling black dogs who ran beside us barking and snapping at the front wheels. When I passed the cemetery it would have taken a minor wrist action to send them off to meet their pals who were waiting at the gate, but the black dogs hugged the wheels as if they had nothing to fear from me. They amused themselves like this until we got to the highway where they lost interest and loped off, real machos with another pointless victory under their collars.

It's a few miles from Dolendo to the lonesome, hypnotic highway that runs from Denver to Texas. I've gotten on that road at night and, forgetting I had a destination, gone right past the Dolendo turnoff, but when you're heading north you meet the interstate before you go too far wrong. The wind blew with fury across the highway, a long-distance wind with Arizona behind it and Texas to go. It was confusing the seasons, swirling snowflakes around, picking up tumbleweeds and slamming them into the car. The howling wind and snow had a female presence, I felt, an angry woman who wanted something from Lonnie, from me. It made me shiver but not with cold, because the Nissan had a good heater and it had gotten warm enough inside for Lonnie to take the sleeping bag off and throw it in the backseat. The defroster cleared the windshield, the wipers ticked. The Japanese import bucked in the wind, but I held on tight. I kept my mind on my driving, my eyes on the road—I wasn't getting any conversation from Lonnie to divert me.

We went under the highway overpass, made a sweeping turn and came up on the interstate right behind a semi with lights of Christmas-tree red, red across the top, down the sides and on the bottom. It seemed like too much trouble to pass him on the windblown highway, so I stayed behind letting the slipstream pull us along.

Not being the kind of person to hold a grudge for more than a few minutes, Lonnie broke her silence. "So, Neil," she said, "you practicing safe sex?"

"Perfecting it."

"Tell me about it."

"What's to tell? Safe sex is an oxymoron."

"You're having safe sex with a moron?"

"You're drunk, Lonnie."

"Not that drunk. Come on, tell me about it, I want to know what *your* sex life is like."

"If you ask me, the whole point of sex is that it isn't safe. That's what makes it interesting."

"There's the feeling that you've gone over the edge and might not come back, that your bones are dissolving. That's pretty interesting," said Lonnie.

"Nature's way of luring you into making babies and preserving the species," I replied.

"The orange whistles and the invisible globes on the other side of death. That's what Rick said."

"Maybe, but García Márquez said it first."

"Well, whoever. Why do they always talk about orgasms as a kind of death when what you're doing could create a life?"

Why indeed?

"Remember that Rolling Stones song 'She Comes in Colors'? Does that ever happen to you, Neil? Do you ever come in colors? Late one night years ago when I was tripping my brains out somewhere I heard an ad for a sofa bed on the radio. 'Spend a lifetime of comfort in the color of your choice,' it said. If you had a choice what would your color be?"

"Right now? Sunshine."

"I'd pick purple, deep violet purple. Whatever else anyone wants to say about Rick, he was a violet lover—the best I've ever had."

One of nature's perverse laws is that you can have the best sex with the worst men. Sometimes there's an inverse correlation between the intensity of the desire and the worthiness of the object. Subconsciously some women are probably attracted to rotten men because it's easier to get out of it, but not Lonnie. She'd stuck it out.

"Would you get married again for really great sex, Neil?" she asked.

"Oh . . . probably not."

"Why not?"

"Because it would break your heart if it didn't last, and if it did you'd never do anything else."

"Who'd want to?" sighed Lonnie. "Neil, there's something I've always wanted to ask you. Now's as good a time as any." She was leaning forward in the semi's red glow, brushing the hair from her face. We'd come upon an incline and the truck was losing speed. The time had come to pull out of the slipstream, get back into the wind and snow. I edged the Nissan into the passing lane.

"Yeah."

"How was it?"

"How was what?"

"You know, sleeping with him."

"Who?" My eyes were on the rearview mirror, waiting for the semi's headlights to appear, signaling me it was safe to cut over. The truck driver flicked his brights, I flicked mine and turned in. Gaudy as they were, I kind of missed having the red lights in front of me. Once they were gone there was nothing to look at but darting, stabbing insects of snow.

"Rick."

"It was fifteen years ago, Lonnie, when I knew Rick."

"But you did sleep with him, didn't you?"

What could I say? I was stoned? He'd talked me into it? We'd been lovers in a previous lifetime with a karmic debt to pay, or, like some people would have, "Well, yeah, but it only happened once so get off my case"? "Yes," I said. "I did."

"So, how was it?"

I didn't remember any whistles or globes. It was an adventure of sorts but it lacked whatever chemistry it takes to make violet purple. "Okay, I guess."

"Just okay?"

It was bad enough I did it, she wanted me to rave about it, too? Sometimes when two women have slept with the same man it creates a rivalry, sometimes a bond, but this had happened so long ago who would expect either? "Everybody slept with everybody in those days, Lonnie, remember? It was a love-in. If it felt good, do it, and if it felt bad, do it anyway. Nobody ever said when, only more. Who knows why? It was hormones, our age, the place, the times, the music."

"Everybody but the Malones . . ."

It was true that the Malones had been known for being faithful.

". . . and me, Neil. Rick was my first and my one and only then. I was seventeen when I went to San Miguel."

I tried to remember Lonnie in those days, La Rubia, the blonde, the girl all the Mexicans wanted. I did some rough calculating and placed her in her early thirties now— younger than I'd thought—which meant she was looking a whole lot older than she should have. She had to look pretty bad at the moment with tears running down her face.

"Lonnie, it wasn't the best thing in the world to do but you and Rick *had* broken up when I slept with him."

"We broke up all the time; it didn't mean anything."

"I didn't know that then."

"I know," she sobbed.

"Then why are you crying?"

"Because my life is turning to shit. Because this time it does mean something. Rick's going to marry shark face."

"Forget about him, Lonnie."

"I can't. He's my soul mate."

How can you be a soul mate, I wondered, with someone who doesn't have a soul? "It seems to me there's been a whole lot of pain for the pleasure. Has it been worth it?"

"Sometimes," she sighed. "Sometimes it has. I need to talk to him, Neil, make him see what he's doing is all wrong."

We'd reached the turnoff to Old Pecos Trail, the scenic route into Santa Fe, and I took it.

"You remember Nemesis, my gray cat?" Lonnie asked.

"Well . . ." Cats and I don't speak the same language. I've never understood what people see in them, and Lonnie had had a whole army since I'd known her. All her cats had the lean, nervous look of strays from the shelter, and I couldn't tell them apart.

"Somebody killed him and left him on my doorstep."

"Are you sure? Maybe it was a dog. Maybe it was natural causes."

"His belly was slit open like that." She ran her finger from her crotch to her chin.

"That's awful."

"It was horrible. His guts were spilled all over. It's just been one crappy thing after another."

I know what it's like to be on a bad-luck roll. A couple of snowflakes stick together at the top of Santa Fe Baldy and by the time they slide to the bottom they've become the avalanche that will squash you. I tried to cheer her up. "It's not all bad. You've got a good job and friends, your car runs."

"Yeah, and that's it. There's only a couple of things to do when I feel like this."

"Valium?" It was a drug Lonnie had always been partial to. Broken hearts, she called them, because they came with a trademark v in the middle that resembled a heart and an indentation where you could break the heart in two.

"I've already done that," she sighed.

"Blues?" I asked. They were ten milligrams. She called the fives mellow yellows.

"Yeah. It's been a blue day but they're just numbing the pain. I'd like to go out to the ruins and meditate."

"You can't go out there now. It's the middle of the night and it's snowing," I said, although actually the snow was letting up and before it had begun to stick to the road, thank God. Tomorrow the sun would come out and the snow would be gone. That's the way the seasons happen around here, winter at night, spring in the morning.

"There's something else, something in Santa Fe that'll make me feel better. I'll show you." She directed me downtown, around the plaza, which was at its best under the street lamps and a dusting of snow. Without cruising low riders and a couple of thousand tourists hanging around, you could get a sense of the past, the moment, maybe, when the Indians chased the Spanish out. You could also see the place clearly now that it was empty: the long, graceful portal in front of the Palace of the Governors, the curving walls of the Fine Arts Museum, the pleasing proportions and soft colors of the rest of the buildings. It was a rare mix of proportion, color and history. At moments like this I understood why people cared so much about preserving the place. Lonnie directed me a few blocks farther to Paloma Street, where we parked in front of a wall. Santa Fe loves walls, soft pastel walls, walls with broken glass embedded in the top, walls that keep the gardens and fountains in, trouble out. This particular wall, lit by a street lamp, was a bunch of gray boards slapped together to hide a construction site.

"There was a beautiful view of the Jemez here before this thing went up," Lonnie said. She looked up and down the empty street, took something from her bag and let herself out of the car.

"What are you doing?" I asked.

"You'll see." She held up a can of spray paint and then she moved it quickly across the wall, spraying in ten-mile orange the large four-letter word: UGLY.

I could have told her that defacing other people's property is a misdemeanor, but they probably didn't take misdemeanors seriously anyway in a city where theft is a fact of life. Besides, the wall *was* ugly. Lonnie posed in front of her graffiti smiling proudly. "You've made your point," I said. "Can we go home now?"

"Why not?" she replied.

Lonnie lived on the West Side in a neighborhood where the front houses come right up to the street and the back houses, reached by narrow driveways, have half a number. Lawyers call themselves *abogados* here and paint murals of conquistadors on their walls, dogs bark all night and your neighbors' brawls sound like they are live in your living room. Her address was 7½ Miranda. I negotiated the street at fifteen miles an hour as you never knew when another car would come around one of the bent-elbow corners that has a house in its crook. The subcompact was the right size for negotiating this street, the wrong one for hitting anything.

"That building is a rape," Lonnie said. "A rape of the most beautiful city in America. They're ruining historic Santa Fe with white bread designs. It's too tall, too wide, too out of proportion, too ugly. You should see the model— it's a goddamn jail."

"They must have gotten approval from the Historic Preservation Board. How?"

"Jorge Mondragon, the chairman, was paid off. They bought him, Neil, and I can prove it." Her eyes had a glittering intensity as she made this statement; I hoped she wouldn't tell me next that the CIA had tapped her phone.

Lonnie's driveway equaled Tim's in ruts. When we got to 7½, I turned off the ignition and surrendered the keys because her house and car keys were on the same ring. She climbed the stoop where the dead Nemesis had been found and opened her front door. One gray cat leaped off the furniture and landed on her, another darted between her legs and ran out the door. "Nemo. Come back here," she yelled at the escapee as it dashed across the stoop and into somebody else's yard.

She handed the first cat, Karma, to me, took a down coat from a hook on the wall and put it on. "I have to go after Nemo, Neil. There's some crazy cat killer out there. Just make yourself at home until I get back. Please don't let Karma get out and keep the curtains closed. Ever since Nemesis was killed, I've had the feeling that someone is watching me."

"Lonnie . . ." A person who kills cats is not a person you want to come across in the middle of the night when you're running on Valium and white zinfandel, but she took off into the shadows behind the main house.

I shut the door, put Karma down, tried to make myself at home, but it didn't come naturally in a place as cluttered as Lonnie's. If you don't have any money, you're better off with a few cheap pieces than a lot of them, but this place looked like she spent her weekends negotiating at the flea market. She had a couple of overstuffed armchairs and an equally stuffed sofa, all covered with Indian bedspreads that hiked up and wrinkled like tight pants on a fat ass. There was a fringed green scarf thrown over a lampshade, giving the room an underwater glow. The obligatory R. C. Gorman print of a mopey woman hung on the wall. The curtains were closed. I went to the kitchen in an aisle that led to the bath to see if I could find something to drink. My foot bumped a box on the floor and made the kitty litter chatter. There were a couple of bottles of white zinfandel in the half-a-refrigerator, a mint seltzer, a six-pack of Tecate, orange juice dated two weeks ago, moldy bean dip, an open package of Ortega tortillas curling at the edges. I picked out a Tecate, popped open the tab and was spotlighted suddenly by a blaze of headlights coming through the window. The lights blinded me but I could tell from their location that it was Lonnie's car and, since she had the keys, no doubt she was in it. She was going somewhere. I was going nowhere until she got back, which convinced me all over again that you should never ever be stuck without your own wheels.

"God damn it, Lonnie," I said.

I went into the living room, picked Karma off the overstuffed sofa, sat down, drank my beer and wondered how long it could take to find a cat that had left tracks in the snow and why you would need a car to do it. By the time I'd finished the beer, there was no sign of Lonnie and I was falling asleep. Lying down on that sofa would be as comfortable as burying your head inside a down pillow. It was covered with gray, white and black cat hair and Karma was doing her best to climb up and leave some more.

I got up, made sure the front door was locked, went into Lonnie's bedroom, sat down on her unmade bed and watched a pink fiberfill comforter slide to the floor. Karma followed me and crawled up on the pillows, purring loudly. Some red petunias on the windowsill leaned out of their pot looking for water. On the bedside table there was a container of mellow yellows and a glass with some pink stuff in it. I opened the drawer, found a fat journal and closed the drawer, having absolutely no desire to read about the soap opera of loving Rick First. There was an afterthought of a room at the back of the house, I remembered. I picked up the comforter and took it with me, shutting the bedroom door to keep Karma in. The room was sort of an attached shed and Lonnie's studio, which she used whenever she had an artistic inclination. There were a few half-finished watercolors leaning against the wall. On a card table I found an old typewriter, some Bic pens and several cans of orange spray paint. A woven Guatemalan hammock hung from the ceiling. It was a summer room, poorly heated and cold, and the screens were still on the windows. Before going to bed I passed through the kitchen into the bathroom. The light switch wasn't in any normal place so I sat down on the toilet seat and peed in the dark. Then I got into the Guatemalan hammock, curled up under the comforter and went to sleep, if you could call it that. The sleep I had didn't say much for Tim's decaf.

Sometime during the night the snow stopped. I woke up noticing that the insulating layer of silence was gone. A woman screamed vile accusations at someone, or was it a monkey screaming at a tree? I was in my hammock in the rain forest at Tikal. I put my hand down to rock myself and an army of red ants ran up my arm. I didn't know it until I laid my head on my arm and the ants ran all over me stinging. I tossed and squirmed, but I was afraid to get up and step on the nest. Something threw itself against the window screen, a monkey with its arms and legs outstretched, or a cat with claws that scratched at the screen. Footsteps crunched on gravel, kitty litter rattled in a box. Snow sagged, melted, dripped, flushed. At the first sign of daylight, I got up, wrapped myself in the comforter, went to the door and watched the yellow-bellied dawn. The sun's early rays coming from behind Santa Fe Baldy lit the undersides of dark, rounded clouds. A neighbor's black dog stuck his head over a wall and barked. A large raven (or was it a crow?) squawked at me from a bare branch. Lonnie's car was not in the driveway. I shut the door, let the comforter drop to the floor, went into the dark bathroom and sat down hard on a cold porcelain bowl. Someone had been here before me and left the toilet seat up.

3

There weren't many places to hide in this house. I checked them all, noticing as I did that the door to Lonnie's bedroom was open. Karma had gotten out and was sleeping on the living room sofa. The boom box and TV were in place. Impossible for me to tell if anything had been taken or if robbery had even been a motive. I took a look at the windows and the door. Except for the room I had slept in the windows were still wrapped tight in plastic, poor people's insulation. The windows in the studio were covered with screens. They would have been easy enough to pry off, but could anyone have come in that way and put a screen back on without my noticing? It was hard to believe I'd slept *that* soundly, when it felt like I hadn't slept at all. The outside door was the kind you lock by turning a button in the knob. An idiot with a credit card and a screwdriver could open it. With the screwdriver you pry loose the strip of wood that is supposed to protect the lock on the outside, insert the credit card, press open the lock. The strip outside Lonnie's lock gave no sign of having been tampered with. She should have gotten herself a deadbolt the minute she moved in here. Santa Fe is devoted to the arts and higher consciousness; it also has more than its share of crimes against women and many of them never get solved. The door was locked when I went to bed; it had been locked when I went out to see the dawn, I remembered turning the button. Whoever had been careless enough to leave the toilet seat up had been careful enough to lock the door on the way out. It was beginning to look like that person had their own key, unless Lonnie had brought somebody home with her and taken them back out again without my hearing. I opened the door and looked carefully at the doorstep and the driveway, which I hadn't when I watched the dawn. There was still a light dusting of snow on the sheltered stoop and it continued for a few feet into the driveway before it had melted or blown away. The tops of the ruts had a cap of snow but by the time you got to Miranda Street there wasn't any snow on the ground at all. The dirt of the driveway was hard and cold enough not to take any prints. There were mixed footprints on the stoop—small ones of a high-heeled boot, Lonnie; medium-size ones of a running shoe, me; and, cutting across the two of us, another larger running shoe that left a series of V impressions like a bird in flight. Lonnie's prints went into the driveway, so did the other's and they both ended at the hard brown dirt. The phone rang and I went inside and answered it. "Hello?" I said.

"Who's this? Neil?"

"Who's asking? Tim?"

"I guess you got home okay."

"More or less."

"I couldn't sleep . . ."

"Me neither."

"So I went out early . . ."

"It's pretty early, Tim, just getting light in fact."

"It's the best time of day if you're up for it. I took a look at your car. Could be a new carburetor you'll be needing."

"How much will that cost me?"

"Three hundred dollars maybe."

"Crap."

"Do you want me to find somebody here or get it towed back to Albuquerque?"

"Tow it," I said.

"Paul at the Citgo station will do it tomorrow if you want."

"Okay, tell him to take it to the flying red horse sign at One Callejon Blanco. Thanks. The guys there will pay him."

"Lonnie up yet?" asked Tim.

"Not to my knowledge."

"Is she all right? She was pretty out of it last night."

"I have no idea. She went out in the middle of the night and hasn't come back."

"Lonnie went out? Where?"

"Beats me."

"You're all alone there?"

"Just me and the cats."

"Well, if you see her tell her I called. Okay?"

"Okay."

"Oh, and Neil. Let me know how you make out with the car."

"Sure. Thanks."

I found some Red Zinger, made myself a cup and sat down in the living room to drink it. I was fed up with Lonnie, sick of the cat hair in her place and hungry for one of Santa Fe's Sunday breakfasts that people wait in line hours for. I went through the closets, found the sweater with the least amount of fur on it and borrowed it. The snow on the stoop was gone when I went out and so were the footprints. A gray cat was sitting on the stoop. I let him in.

It was the kind of morning Santa Fe does well: blue sky, clear air; brisk, but not freezing; the aroma of piñon burning that you smell in the street, but seldom in your fireplace; white snow topping brown adobe and melting softly; mist rising from the pavement. I walked downtown and beat the morning crowd to Pasqual's, and had fresh orange juice and huevos rancheros with wake-up green chile.

I circled the plaza—the Pueblo Indians were just beginning to set their wares up under the portal—and went into the lobby of the library to use the pay phone, but somebody had beaten me to it. While I waited I examined a bulletin board that listed places for rent, rides east and west and New Age workshops. There was Jungian dream analysis, journal keeping, meditation, astrology, tarot, massage, being a woman—you were required to bring a pillow and a blanket to that one. A guy wearing jeans, boots and a cowboy hat looked at the notices with me, waiting for the phone, too. He was thin and wiry and had eyes of faraway blue. His hands were stained from work, I noticed: a cowboy, or a sculptor maybe who worked in hard-edged metals and wood.

"That's a little misleading, don't you think?" He pointed to a notice for a "freeing up" weekend workshop that cost $250.

"I guess you've got to find some way to make a living in Santa Fe," I replied. "I understand who gives these things, but who pays to go to them?"

"There are a lot of rich people here."

"A number of poor ones, too."

"There's a big difference between them. Here's one where you might get something for your money, anyway, a raffle with a chance to win a Mustang. One out of fifty—

that's not too terrible. A new car or enlightenment, what'll it be?"

"I could use a new car myself."

"Maybe you need a car before you can become enlightened."

"Maybe my car needs to be enlightened."

The woman stepped out of the phone booth. "The phone has just been freed up," I said.

"That'll be $250," he replied.

I laughed. "Go ahead, you first," he told me.

"If you insist," I said.

I called the Kid and was happy to find him at home and awake. In the background Mexican music played loudly, the way he liked it.

"Kid," I said. "I'm in Santa Fe. My car broke down last night so I came into town with my friend Lonnie and spent the night at her place. I think it's the carburetor."

"Don't worry, Chiquita, I fix it. It take two, three days maybe to get the parts."

"I'll have it towed to your shop tomorrow, but in the meantime I'm going to need a car."

"I pick you up if you want, take you to work in the morning."

"Thanks, Kid. Maybe I should just rent one up here. I'm going to need one to get around during the day anyway."

"Okay. See you later?"

"Yup."

Before I freed up the phone booth for the cowboy sculptor, I tried Lonnie's number. If anyone heard it ringing, they didn't let me know.

The Inn at Loreto has a rental-car booth in the lobby, and in their parking lot, which they charge to get into in the tourist season, are a number of Fords from the Rich Ford Agency, the rental car of choice in northern New Mexico. The one they gave me had an automatic transmission, air conditioning and a working radio. I didn't need the air conditioning yet, but you always need a radio. It was tuned to the golden oldie station, and "Bony Moronie" was the first song to come out of the speakers. I wouldn't want to get any older than that. I fastened my seat belt and adjusted the rearview mirror and the one on the side that said OB-JECTS IN MIRROR ARE CLOSER THAN THEY APPEAR.

I crossed town on Alameda, went by Lonnie's and took a look down her long, empty driveway. If she'd returned, she'd gone out again. The old part of Santa Fe, east and west, has the kind of closed, turned-inward feeling of a desert city, walled to keep the infidel out, and I felt like one here: a cynic, a nonbeliever, uninterested in raising consciousness or money. I was glad to get out of the narrow streets and onto Cerrillos, the fast-food strip that could be Anywhere, U.S.A. Here I felt at home. I watched for the ARRIBA TACOS sign with flames licking at the red letters; they have the best drive-in sopapillas in America. I pulled up at the window and bought two with meat to save for dinner.

I continued on Cerrillos till I reached the interstate, then turned south into the wide open spaces, home of the big thoughts, but the thoughts I had today were not major. I worried about my car, wondered where Lonnie had gone, watched the clouds as they formed in the sky. There were some lenticulars—the falcons of the cloud world—hanging on over Ortiz Mountain. Lenticular means lens shaped, but these clouds, formed by air breaking over mountains, have a sinuous elegance that looks more like wings than lenses to me. Higher up, a jet had left a squiggly trail in the sky of deep-water blue, so blue that when I got to the top of La Bajada, I wanted to dive in. Climbing that hill, I got stuck behind a truck spewing a trail of black exhaust from its diesels. Exhaust is at its ugliest where the air is the clearest.

I stepped on the gas, pulled into the passing lane. There was a pause and I had to wait for the automatic passing gear to click in. In high school we called a car like this a legger, poky as a dog that stops, lifts its leg and pees at every tree. The hesitation was annoying, but there were lots of junkers on the road and I was able to do my share of passing between La Bajada and Bernalillo. A lot of the cars I overtook had orange polyester Garfields hanging on the window by their suction paws, grinning stupidly at me. After Santo Domingo Pueblo I came upon Budaghers, an exit leading nowhere that the highway department authorized because someday somebody's rich developer relative might want to build there. By the time I got to Bernalillo I had entered billboard country. There was a new one advertising North America's biggest Indian powwow and an old one with a drive-in-movie-size picture of Ron Bell, Attorney. "I sue drunk drivers," Ron says, next to a glass with a red line through it. In another week you start seeing pilgrims alongside the highway as they hike to the Santuario de Chimayo eighty miles north, where, on Good Friday, people from all over northern New Mexico give thanks for their blessings and apologize for their sins. They call them pilgrims here, but I prefer the Spanish word, *peregrinos*.

At Montgomery I got off I-25 and went home to La Vista to face a refrigerator that was even emptier than Lonnie's. There were two six-packs of Tecate and a couple of limes on the shelves. I added the sopapillas. The Kid wasn't expected till dinnertime and I hadn't had any sleep that I could remember so I lay down on the bed. Fran Lebowitz said that sleep is death without the responsibility, and naps are sleep without the responsibility. I was just about to leave responsibility behind when the phone rang.

"Yeah," I answered.

It was a guy with a pleading, pathetic voice who wanted to lick somebody's pussy. "Please," he begged.

"Fuck you," I said.

I hung up, then reconsidered, took the phone off the hook

and left it that way. It went through a sixty-second buzz to tell me it was off the hook, but I already knew that. When the buzzing stopped, I slept the deep sleep of the irresponsible until the Kid pounded on the door.

It didn't feel like the beginning of spring anymore, but it's always good to see the Kid. We don't see each other enough for things to get stale—that's the way we like it. I served him a cold Tecate with lime and salt and heated the sopapillas in the oven; I don't have a microwave. My sopapilla was all I had expected: a light crust, chunks of potato and meat, shreds of tomato and lettuce, sauce that was almost hot enough to cry for. The Kid took a bite and made a face.

"Chiquita, where did you get these?"

"Santa Fe. Why?"

"There's something wrong with mine, the meat feels funny like a *caracol* or something."

"Let me see." I took a bite. It had the hot taste of the sauce, but the texture was, just like he said, slimy as a snail. It was something that has the taste of whatever you put it in, but a texture all its own. "Tofu," I said.

"What's that?"

"Something they eat in Santa Fe. They make it from soybeans; it's supposed to be good for you."

"Why they do that to beans?"

"Who knows? Arriba Tacos is serving vegetarian food now. They must have put this one in by mistake. I'll trade with you, Kid, I can eat tofu if it's disguised well enough."

"Okay," he said.

The Kid slept over and we made cautious love. In the morning he went to the shop and I drove the rental car to my office on Lead in a frame and stucco building that not too long ago was somebody's house. HAMEL AND HARRISON, LAW OFFICES, the sign says, me and my partner Brinkley

Harrison. Brink and my secretary, Anna, eating their breakfast at Anna's desk, had noticed me pull into the driveway in the white Rich Ford.

"New car?" asked Brink, blinking his eyes and raising his eyebrows, gestures he makes so often it's obvious *he* isn't worried about getting lines in his face. What's one more wrinkle in an unmade bed? Brink was dressed for failure in a baggy-around-the-knees gray suit, a shirt that could be white again if someone threw a little bleach at it and a tie with last night's dinner on it. As part of a role change taking place right now men are learning to cook, tidy up after themselves and keep their clothes clean. There was a time when it would have been said that Brink needed a woman to take care of him. I'd say he needed himself, but what I thought wasn't news to Brink.

Anna had dressed for spring in a black leather miniskirt, black pantyhose with arrows pointing to her ankles, high-heeled black shoes, blood red fingernails. They were eating Egg McMuffins from McDonald's with green chile on the side.

"Brink, if I were buying a new car would I buy a white Ford with an automatic transmission?" I asked.

"I'd buy a red Trans Am if it was me," said Anna.

"Whose car is that and where is yours?" asked Brink, who liked to consider my life his.

"The car belongs to Dollar Rental. Mine is in Dolendo waiting to be towed back here. I think it needs a new carburetor."

"Uh-oh." Brink looked worried.

"When did you get home?" asked Anna.

"Yesterday."

"What you been up to since then?"

"Sleeping. Why?" This was a lot of curiosity for Anna, who took no interest in my life at all.

"Your phone's off the hook."

"Oh, God, I forgot. No wonder I slept so well."

"Tim Malone's been trying to get in touch with you. It's important, he says." She handed me a pink slip that said, "Call Tim M. ASAP."

"Who's that?" Brink's eyebrows went up again. "A client?"

"A friend of mine from San Miguel, remember?"

"Oh, yeah," said Brink. "Him."

"I heard a new lawyer joke this weekend," said Anna, who collected them. "What's brown and tan and looks good on a lawyer?"

"An attaché case?" asked Brink, who should have known better.

"A pit bull," she said.

"Ha, ha," I replied, going into my office and shutting the door. I called Tim and got a recorded message that said, "This is the Malone answering machine, you know what to do."

"This is Neil. I'm at the office. You've got the number."

It was a morning, like most mornings at Hamel and Harrison, filled with events that neither alter nor illuminate the times: real estate closings, divorces. There are lawyers in large "prestigious" firms who specialize in these areas, but why anybody would do that beats me. At noon I had a lunch date with a client and drove across town to André's. I guess they served *nouvelle cuisine* because the cilantro chicken with tomatillos was delicious and twenty minutes later I was hungry again. I was nibbling on M&Ms at my desk when Tim called back at two. "Brace yourself, Neil," he said, "I've got some bad news."

"Let's see, the Rabbit was being towed and fell off the hitch on the way to Albuquerque, somebody hit it and they're going to sue."

He didn't laugh. "It's bad, Neil. You'd better sit down to hear this."

"I'm sitting."

"Lonnie's dead," he said.

"What?"

"She's dead."

"She can't be dead. I just saw her. She was all right."

"Her body was found Sunday morning by a man walking his dog at the ruins."

"The ruins? She went there?"

"We were hoping you might know why."

"She said she wanted to go out there and meditate, but I didn't take her seriously; it was snowing, it was the middle of the night. She's really dead?"

"Yes."

"Oh God. I don't believe it."

"Shit happens, Neil."

"If it happened Sunday morning, then why didn't somebody call me sooner?"

"Believe me we tried. Your phone was off the hook."

"I had an obscene call and forgot to put it back. How did she die?"

"A lethal combination of drugs and alcohol, the police think. They're leaning toward suicide."

"Suicide? That's ridiculous. She wasn't suicidal."

"Tell *them* that. Since you were probably the last person to see her alive, they want to talk to you. Detective Railback is going to call. The body will be cremated, but we're going to have a wake at her house at noon tomorrow, can you come?"

"Of course. Is there anything I can do?"

"Just be here tomorrow."

"I will," I said.

I buzzed Anna on the intercom. "Something came up and I have to go to Santa Fe tomorrow. If a Detective Railback calls, make an appointment for me in the morning. Tell anybody else I'll call them back."

"You got it," she said. Sometimes Anna's lack of curiosity is a blessing. Lonnie's death wasn't news I wanted to share with anyone—not even the Kid—just yet. Like a mantling bird protecting its prey, I wanted to wrap my wings around this disaster, stare at it and keep it to myself. I put my head down on the desk for a while and when I looked up I began drawing lines of Vs like flying birds across a yellow legal pad. I waited for Anna and Brink to leave at five and a little while later I left, too. Among the messages on Anna's desk was one that said my appointment with Detective Michael Railback was at ten tomorrow. I drove to Roosevelt Park, sat on the grass and watched the bare-limbed cottonwoods shadow the ground like lines on a map, rivers seen from the air, or veins. A voice on a loudspeaker drifted over from the stadium. "Down on the infield," it said, and then "Will everybody please help set up the hurdles." I sat on the grass until dark and then I went to Souper Salad on Central. Ignoring the salad bar, I went directly to the baked potatoes, took one from the warming tray, put it in a Styrofoam box, poured cheese sauce all over it. It was the kind of food mothers make, comfort food.

When I got home I took my old friend Cuervo Gold out, put some ice in a glass, poured the Gold over the ice. I have a box of black cherry jello that I keep in the cupboard for bad days. I mixed the jello, added another ice cube for quick setting and put it in the refrigerator. I turned the oven to warm, put the baked potato in. Then I took my boom box and a tape into the bathroom, ran a hot bath, poured in some foaming oil. I sat in the tub, smoked Marlboros and listened to Marianne Faithfull's broken English voice singing about heroes who smiled as they killed and "Why D'Ya Do It." By the time I got out of the bath, the tape had run through and dinner was ready. I ate—soggy potato, sticky jello. It was food, but there wasn't much comfort in it. I had a cup of Sleepytime tea, went to bed and lay there staring at the strip of light that comes in where the drapes don't meet and tracks across the ceiling.

I watched the light and when it met a faraway point I dreamed about cats. They're a powerful symbol, even to those of us who avoid them. I was in a high-rise building somewhere in my dream and a cat was clinging to the window screen. Something kept me from moving; I knew I should get up, had to get up, but I couldn't do it, couldn't let the cat in. It went on clawing and clawing until it fell.

4

Driving up I-25 in the morning I watched gray clouds and virga over the Jemez Mountains. Virga is a phenomenon of dry climates, precipitation that evaporates before it reaches the ground. It hangs over the thirsty mountains like a dream that will never come true.

The police station is at the limits of Santa Fe, conveniently near the interstate. It's got a trailer park on one side of it and a shopping mall on the other, and the flags of New Mexico and the U.S. wave over the door. Although I represent clients in Santa Fe from time to time I had never had the pleasure of meeting Detective Michael Railback. While I waited for him, I read yesterday's *New Mexican*, which someone had left lying around the lobby. Lonnie was on the front page smiling like the prom queen she'd never been. A La Luz man named Pete Vigil found the body in a cave around eight on Sunday morning while walking at the ruins, I read. Lonnie's car had been parked off the road and was concealed by piñons. Had it been left in a visible spot, someone might have noticed and found her sooner. The victim had been seen at a party earlier in the evening drinking heavily, the newspaper said. The apparent cause of death was a combination of drugs and alcohol. When no one was looking, I ripped the article out and took it.

Then I watched the police walk through the grim and depressing lobby; there wasn't anything else to look at. They moved stiffly in their law enforcement suits, holsters slapping, pant legs rustling together. There was no way you could sneak up behind someone in an outfit like that. Railback was ready eventually and I was directed to his office down the hall.

The detective sat at his desk in civilian clothes. He never got up, so I could only estimate how tall he was—not very, I'd say; he had the overdeveloped upper body of a short man in a macho job. His hair was trim, his smile was bright, his brown eyes lit up when they saw my Ray-Ban sunglasses.

"Ray-Bans. How long have you had those?"

I thought a moment. "Ten years maybe. They were too expensive to lose."

"Ray-Bans never wear out and people keep them forever. Those metal frames get bent a lot, though, don't they?"

"Yeah, they do." He hadn't offered me a seat, so I helped myself.

"I like to straighten 'em. It's a hobby. You want me to fix yours?"

What could I say? My eyes had become a road map and I didn't want anybody looking for a destination in them? "Go ahead," I replied, handing over the Ray-Bans.

He took tweezers from his drawer, played around with the frames, held them up to my face, adjusted the nose pads, held them up again. I know detectives like to act goofy to make people feel at ease and let their guard down, but Railback was taking it too far. Eventually, he was either satisfied by the way the Ray-Bans fit or had seen enough of the red in my eyes. "They're okay now," he said, handing the glasses back to me. "You have pretty eyes. Why do you cover them up?"

"I see better in shades," I replied, hooking the glasses over my ears. The pads no longer pinched my nose and the Ray-Bans felt a lot better, I'll admit it. I looked out the window behind him at the MERVYN's sign and the traffic going by on Cerrillos while Railback consulted his file. "So you were the last person to see Lonnie Darmer alive Saturday night."

"I saw her Saturday night. I wouldn't say I was the last person who did."

"Since we haven't found anyone else. Why don't you tell me what happened?"

With the exception of the "ugly" on the wall episode I told him. When I'd finished, I asked what had killed her.

"According to the medical director's report, a combination of drugs and alcohol. We're leaning toward suicide." He began picking up paper clips on his desk with the tweezers and dropping them again.

"It wasn't a suicide."

"How do you know?" The paper clips pinged when they hit the desk.

"She wasn't suicidal when I saw her." People who have dreams don't commit suicide, I thought, and her dream was to stop the Ugly Building. But I didn't tell him that.

"You did say she was crying over her ex-husband."

"She's been crying about him for years. It wasn't anything to commit suicide over. Believe me."

"You never know what will set someone off. Sometimes it only takes one little thing."

"Did you find a suicide note?"

"Nope, but that doesn't mean anything; lots of times we don't." He put the tweezers down, looked at a sheet of paper on his desk. "Well, I guess that does it, you're the last person on my list."

"You're telling me that this is the end of your investigation?"

"We haven't got anything to investigate. A thirty-three-year-old woman commits suicide, that's no crime."

"How will you know if you don't investigate?" I said.

"The body showed nothing a policeman could take to the bank: no defense wounds, no trauma, no scratches, no needle marks, nothing but some bruises on her thighs that were probably caused by rough consensual sex."

"Rough consensual sex?"

"That's it."

"What's the difference between bruises caused by rough consensual sex and bruises caused by rape?"

"There's no way of telling for sure. But she was neatly dressed and covered up, there were no other marks on her, no evidence of resistance, no evidence of rape. Having sex isn't a crime. Our theory is that she had it earlier in the evening, was depressed—you've confirmed that—went to the ruins by herself, took Valium, drank wine, died." He began picking up paper clips and prepared to dismiss me. "Anything else?"

"You haven't told me about the crime scene. What did that show?" I certainly wouldn't be the first to accuse the Santa Fe Police Department of a cavalier attitude about certain crimes. For a city of fifty-five thousand people it's had more than its share of unsolved murders of women. It's been said that the police are overworked and badly trained, that there is no incentive to excel, that the pay sucks. Whatever the cause, police have been known to screw up crime scenes. The night a woman named Teri Mulvaney was murdered twenty-eight of them entered her bedroom and somehow both the body and the phone ended up in different positions than they had started out in. When the time came to prosecute there was no evidence to do it with.

"The scene showed that a woman crawled into a cave alone, lay down and died," said Railback. "Period. Amen. There was an empty container of Valium in her pocket. No evidence that anyone went there with her."

"Someone came into her house that night."

"You mean because of the . . . toilet seat?" He smiled. "It couldn't be that it was up before you got there or that you did it yourself accidentally?"

"No, it couldn't."

"Maybe someone was visiting *you.*"

"No, they weren't."

"Maybe someone she knew stopped by. It's not a crime to urinate indoors either, and you said yourself there was no sign of breaking and entering. We'll be in touch if we do investigate because you were the last person known to have seen Lonnie Darmer alive. But right now we've got no evidence, no crime." The meeting was over, even though Railback remained stuck to his chair. Was it arrogance, ignorance or laziness that kept him from getting up? I wondered. His way of treating me like a modern woman or was it just because he was short?

I found my own way out, got the rental car and drove to Lonnie's for the wake. The interview made me late and I had to park way down Miranda Street. I pulled up onto the sidewalk to get out of the way and walked to 7½ alongside one of those adobe-colored walls that Santa Fe loves. Between the cars on the sidewalk and the wall, there was barely enough room for me. With all the cars here and in the driveway and the yellow Nissan parked at the head of the line, you could almost convince yourself that Lonnie was throwing a party, a wedding instead of a wake. The house was jammed full and at times the place had an excited party noise, maybe because the cast from Tim's party was there, or maybe that's just the way people act when they get together around food and drink. The social instincts are pretty strong, and so is the urge to consume when faced with the unexplainable and the grim. It was lunchtime and people had brought food, which was spread out all over the kitchen along with a number of bottles, a coffee urn and a fair amount of beer. Some people waited until afternoon to start drinking, some didn't. Old habits resurface quickly at times like this.

Tim was standing in the kitchen holding a glass of something I could see right through. "Perrier?" I asked.

"A martini," said Tim. "A silver bullet. I feel like shit, Neil."

"I know, darlin'." I hugged him.

His eyelids were red and crusty and appeared to be walking away from his eyes. "Why? Can you just tell me that?" he asked.

"No," I said.

Jamie, who was seldom at Tim's side in a crowd, happened to be standing nearby talking to Ci. Ci had the Santa Fe look, a gauzy white dress, a silver concho belt and long turquoise earrings. I didn't often notice what Jamie wore, just her expressions, which were usually serene like she was listening to some inner music. Today she looked as if the music had stopped and she was wearing an UGLY button pinned to a dark blue dress.

"Have you got another one of those?" I asked her.

She pulled one out of her purse and handed it to me. I pinned it to my waist.

"Neil, right?" asked Ci.

"Ci," I replied.

"The death experience is a very powerful time. Lonnie has made the transition, gone to be with the being of light."

"Why did it have to happen now?" Jamie sighed. It was Ci's cue to say that we all choose the moment of our death, but Jamie didn't give her a chance. "The Darmers are in the living room. I'm sure they'd like to see you, Neil."

"Good idea," I said and went into the living room to pay my respects. Someone had vacuumed and straightened the place up. The gray cats, one each, had taken possession of the armchairs before any mourners could. The Darmers, who were sitting on the sofa under the melancholy R. C. Gorman print, held hands. Lonnie's father was weathered, thin with the tensile strength of a man who'd worked outdoors, a carpenter, maybe, or a lineman. The mother was Lonnie thirty years down the road, if her daughter had gone down that road. She was the father's opposite and complement, round and soft—in her case voluptuousness *had* become fat—with thin, bleached hair and too much makeup. It wasn't clear yet where her strength would come from. What could you say to people who had just lost their daughter? Up close I could see how devastated they were. There was a glaze over their eyes but behind it a hungry beast waited. "Mr. and Mrs. Darmer, I'm so . . . so sorry . . ."

"Bunny and Arthur, please," said Bunny, taking my hand.

"Neil Hamel," I replied.

"Aren't you Lonnie's friend who's a lawyer in Albuquerque?" she said.

"Yes." I searched for something to say and came up with "That was such a nice picture in the paper," but it sounded stupid, even to me.

"My beautiful, beautiful girl." Bunny gripped my hand tight, looking all the way into the back of my eyes and then she released me. "Thanks for coming."

Others were waiting to see them, so I excused myself and went into the bedroom. The bed had been made and I sat down on top of the pink comforter. There were a bunch of people in the room, talking softly; nobody was paying any attention to me. The bottle of Valium was gone from the bedside table, I noticed. The petunias had climbed back into their po⋅ —apparently they'd found some water. I opened the drawer in the bedside table. It was empty. The journal that had been here before was gone.

I got up and went into the studio, where Tim stood staring at the card table and a couple was sitting on the hammock. It was large enough, a matrimonial, as it is called in Guatemala, a swinging bed for two. "I slept there Saturday," I said to Tim, indicating the hammock, "and spent a rotten night with strange dreams and weird sounds. I thought the problem was your coffee at first, but . . ." Not having decided whether to tell him about the toilet seat or not, I was letting the conversation wander to see where it ended up, but it made no difference to Tim. He wasn't listening anyway.

"What's *he* doing here?" he asked, looking out the window at someone who was coming up the driveway. Rick First.

"I assume because he was involved with Lonnie for most of her adult life and was once married to her."

"Well, he's not anymore," said Tim, "and he's got no right to be here."

It was inevitable in a house as small and crowded as this that we'd all run into each other. It didn't bother me to see Rick. What had gone down between us wasn't much to begin with and took place so long ago that it seemed like it had happened to someone else in another lifetime. Reincarnation without the responsibility.

I went to the living-room doorway and watched Rick's back while he waited to talk to the Darmers. His jeans had neat dry cleaner creases, I noticed. Maybe he'd kept the pressing habit from San Miguel, where the maids put creases in everything, even your underwear. Rick's shirt was blue and white stripes of expensive cotton. His hair was shorter and neater and had gotten gray. Lonnie hadn't told me that. I watched him take a comb from his hip pocket while he waited and run it through his hair. When he finished, he looked at the comb, pulled out the gray hairs that had gotten caught in the fine teeth and dropped them to the floor. I saw the Darmers stiffen when they noticed he was next. It was a moment that even I didn't want to eavesdrop on, so I went into the kitchen and waited, certain that Rick's next stop would be the bar.

"Neil, boy do I ever need a drink," he said when he showed up in a few minutes. He had what Lonnie called robin's-egg-blue eyes, flecked with brown like the eggshells. They had always been strange and striking, and were even more so now that his hair had turned gray, pale hair, pale eyes. It was enough to make you wonder if he'd dyed it—if anybody makes gray dye. His face hadn't changed much, it was smooth as ever. Some people thought Rick was handsome and maybe he was, but his mouth was small and closed and rarely had any expression, except when he laughed and revealed a pair of oversized canines. He hadn't gotten flabby, however, I'd give him credit for that. He poured himself some vodka, drank it down. "Lonnie's dead. It sucks, doesn't it?" He poured another shot, held up the bottle. "One for you?"

"Got one, thanks."

"The Cuervo Gold Kid." He smiled a slight, closed-lip smile. "You haven't changed much."

"Only on the inside," I said. "You've changed quite a bit."

"Success," he said earnestly. "It does a lot for a person."

"Really?"

"I'm involved in a terrific project, one that will make my career. The First Building. And I'm getting married again."

"Congratulations."

"To a wonderful woman. Marci Coyle."

"So I've been told. Tell me, what do *you* think happened to Lonnie?"

"She was drinking heavily, took too much Valium, a lethal combination." He shrugged. "Wasn't that what the police said?"

"That's what they said. Why was she at the ruins?"

"She liked to go out there and meditate. Sometimes I went with her when we were together, but usually she went by herself. You know the cave that has the water bearer carved in it? She thought it was a power spot."

"She went there alone at night?" New Age meditation music had been playing quietly in the background, but someone turned the volume up and Aretha Franklin began to sing—loud—about some no-good heartbreaker.

Rick raised his voice to get it over the music. "Yeah. Lonnie wasn't the most careful person in the world. You know that, Neil. She just never got her act together and that's what finally ruined it for us. We'd still be married today if she had quit the substance abuse. Well, I've got to get going. It was good to see you." He looked at his watch and as his eyes traveled downward toward the numbers on his wrist he happened to notice the UGLY button pinned on me. "Jesus Christ, you, too? Why do people have to wear those? I don't understand why everyone is so opposed to the building."

"It *is* going to be rather large."

"It's a meaningful balancing and articulation of mass, it has the classic look of puddled adobe, it interfaces well with the neighborhood. It pisses me off that no one is willing to give us a chance. You haven't even seen the model, have you?"

Only the wall, but I didn't tell him that.

"You really ought to look at something before you go around campaigning against it. We're having a party at the office Thursday to show the model to prospective tenants. Why don't you come?"

"I just might," I said. The music had changed to Patsy Cline's tear-jerking man-that-got-away songs: "I Fall to Pieces," "Your Cheatin' Heart," "She's Got You" and finally "Sweet Dreams" with a broken-hearted catch in her voice. Patsy poured out her heart in that one. She could do it if anybody could; loving a shit was something she knew all about. If anybody ever sang or wrote a moving song about being happily married I'd yet to hear it. Patsy Cline was a country-and-western singer in the fifties and early sixties. Lonnie loved her sad songs, especially when she was in a funk about Rick. Like a lot of the greats, Patsy died young. We (Rick, me, Tim, Jamie and just about everybody else at the wake) belonged to a generation of dead heroes and prolonged adolescence—you have to wonder sometimes about the connection.

Rick stopped talking about himself just long enough to let the music sink in. "Patsy Cline? Who would play *that* at a wake?"

"Me," said Tim, who had surfaced beside us.

"It's totally uncalled for," Rick snapped.

"Nope. It's exactly what *is* called for."

While the two of them stood nose to nose like rams in rut glaring at each other and pawing the ground, I looked down at their feet. Both were shod in running shoes. Rick's were a pair of brand-new black high-top Reeboks, Tim's were Adidas retreads, mud brown, with holes where the fabric was supposed to connect with the leather.

"You're the reason we're all here today. Lonnie died because of you," said Tim, swaying slightly and staring at Rick accusingly with his wide open newborn's eyes.

"Lonnie died because she was a substance abuser," Rick replied, stiff as a stick.

Tim poked his finger into Rick's chest, a few sips away from giving him a shove.

Rick stepped back. "Don't make me hit you, Tim."

"Nobody's going to be hitting anybody," said Jamie, whose antennae were ever alert to Tim in trouble. She took his arm. "We're going home, darling."

"I'm not finished yet," Tim said.

"Yes, you are. Let's go."

Tim looked into his drink as if he wanted to throw it in Rick's face, but he put it down and let Jamie lead him away. "I'll settle with you later," he said.

"What got into him?" asked Rick, watching Tim and Jamie blend into the crowd.

"He cared about Lonnie," I replied.

"We all did."

"Right."

"So what's Tim doing these days? Still writing poetry?" Rick smiled a tight-lipped little smile.

"Yes," I said.

"Some people never grow up."

And some people grow up to be assholes, I thought, jerks mature into pricks, hippies become yuppies. It's not often that anybody improves with age, and when they do it takes a long, long time. It's easier to be good when you're very young or very old than in all the sloppy, conflicted years between.

Rick looked at his digital watch again. "Two o'clock. Jesus, I've got to get going. Good seeing you, Neil. I hope you'll come on Thursday."

"Good-bye, Rick," I replied. I hung around the kitchen a little longer, wondering what had possessed me to sleep with him and what had made Lonnie so obsessed with him. I made myself a ham and cheese sandwich for the road and put it in a plastic Baggie that I found under the sink. I put another plastic bag in my pocket, and then I took off, too.

On my way out I stopped at Lonnie's yellow Nissan heavy with bumper stickers: NEW MEXICO NATIVE, STOP THE UGLY BUILDING, DON'T BUY EXXON, WHIP WIPP, BETTER ACTIVE TODAY THAN RADIOACTIVE TOMORROW. I took a look inside. There was a blanket fuzzy with cat hair on the backseat, but no sleeping bag. The Darmers could have taken it out or put it in the trunk.

"Hi." The voice took me by surprise as I hadn't heard anybody coming. A blond-haired, bright-eyed teenager stood at my left. He was a cute kid and women had probably gooed all over him in supermarkets and malls when he was little. Maybe they still did; he had that look of an eager stray that some women can't resist. Like everybody else he was wearing running shoes. Sometimes it makes me long for the days when people wore Frye boots that weighed five pounds each; at least they let you know when they were coming. Neither a cholo nor a UNM student, the teenager was wearing a plain yellow T-shirt, shabby but neat.

"Hello," I replied.

"Wow. Lot of cars here," he said.

"Lot of people, too."

"You been inside?"

"Yup."

"You must be a friend of Lonnie's." The boy's fingers drummed on the roof of the Nissan.

"I was." Compared to *him* an old friend.

"I'd like to go in, but I'm not a friend like you. I mean I knew her, but not like a friend, if you know what I mean."

He wasn't exactly articulate, but what could you expect from a cute teenager? "Actually, I don't know what you mean."

"I live over there." He pointed across the wall to a garage-size adobe hovel. "With my mom. She knows the guy who owns this place. Sometimes I work around here and help Lonnie out—did, I mean, I guess. She's kind of messy." He gave a tidy person's shiver of distaste.

"You knew Lonnie, you can go in."

"You mean it?"

"Why not?"

"Why not? Okay. Thanks. Hey, there's Ci."

Ci had come out the door and was standing on the stoop watching us. "Hello, Dolby," she said.

"Dolby?" I said. "Your name is Dolby?"

"That's right," he grinned. "I got that name because I sound good."

"Dolby, you are going to help me out tomorrow, aren't you?" said Ci, walking toward us.

"Hey, why not?" said Dolby.

I didn't especially want to talk to Ci, so I said good-bye and left.

5

It was about two-fifteen in the afternoon; there was nothing I had, or wanted, to get back to Albuquerque for, so I drove out to the ruins to see for myself if there was any evidence of a crime. I got on St. Francis, which joins up with highways 84 and 285, the routes north. It also happens to be the road the federal government intends to use to transport nuclear waste through Santa Fe to its burying ground in southern New Mexico, the Waste Isolation Pilot Project, known as WIPP. The people who lived and worked twenty feet from the proposed truck route didn't like it much; they'd put out signs that said so.

The road begins to climb when it reaches the white crosses of the National Cemetery. To be buried next to the highway under a white wooden cross is not a bad way to end up, but I'd rather be off by myself somewhere than in a cemetery. On the back road to Chimayo there's a wooden cross with a white circle around it and a white scarf waving from it like a Buddhist prayer flag. It sits on a knoll surrounded by sky, which beats having your ashes blowing back in the window of somebody's airplane. I didn't want to think about what the Darmers would do with Lonnie's ashes, but that's exactly what I was thinking about. She had had a mystical attachment to the ruins; it would be the logical place to scatter her ashes—if she had chosen to die there. Her death was a knot that I was struggling to untie. *If* was the loop at the center of the knot.

My rental car took the hill like the legger it was, pissing at every piñon; I got stuck in the slow lane, passed and passed again. It gave me lots of time to appreciate the view. The east was layered with colors: golden green piñons, plum-colored mountains whose snowcapped peaks pushed at the limits of white, above them blue sky and white clouds streaked with watercolor gray. At the top of the rise a sign says ELEVATION 7500 FEET and a wide bare view opens up to the north. You see piñons, mesas, mountains one hundred and fifty miles away in Colorado, sky. It's one of those places where you get the feeling that God speaks; you just hope he's not calling your name.

The downhill stretch forced me to keep my eyes on the road and my mind on my driving. It is one of the more beautiful sections of road around here (beauty being a matter of degree in New Mexico). It's also one of the more dangerous, but that's a matter of degree as well. There's a concrete divider to keep you from mixing it up with the oncoming traffic, but the divider isn't something you'd want to make contact with either. It's a wall, oppressive and ugly, limiting the room to maneuver. The legger was picking up speed faster than the truck ahead of me so I squeezed into the passing lane. There's no inspection in New Mexico, no rust either, and vehicles live forever. The truck I passed was an ancient Chevrolet Apache with a mouth full of chrome. It wouldn't get far in the Taos ugly truck contest—too well taken care of, newly painted turquoise, smooth and rounded as adobe—but it might win a prize for the number of people in the cab. I counted four before my exit appeared and I had to focus my attention on turning off.

I headed into cave country, into the mesas carved by volcanoes a million years ago. The cliffs here are the pinkish color of Anglo skin with natural indentations that were enlarged into dwellings. People lived in these cliffs for centuries and the ruins are one of the places they settled. The caves there face south to provide warmth in the winter, shade in the summer, and there was a wash that flowed through the valley for water. It was a simple and beautiful way to live and no one has ever been able to explain why the ruins were abandoned. It happened before the conquest, so it's one thing that can't be blamed on the conquerors.

I drove up the winding road and pulled into the parking lot, an unmarked gravel spot. Unless you had hawk eyes or a guide, you'd never find it. To some people that was what made the ruins special, only a select few knew where they were. They are on privately owned land and are fenced, but that hasn't kept anyone in the know out yet. I parked the car, the only one there, which was how I'd hoped it would be. The ideal way to get here would be on foot or to hitchhike, because a parked car told others where the ruins were and sooner or later one of them was liable to join you, unless, of course, you were like Lonnie and hid your car. But with a car like the legger there was always the possibility you wouldn't get it back out.

I checked the clock over the rental-car mirror—two forty-five. It had taken me a half hour to get here. Lonnie left me around midnight, Pete Vigil found the body at eight. Factoring in traveling time, that left seven and a half hours. What else had she done? Where had she gone? To a bar? To see Rick? Or was Railback right? Had she just come here and swallowed Valium? Then where had she gotten the "rough consensual" bruises?

Before entering the ruins, I walked down the road and found the spot where the Nissan had been parked—a distance, I guessed, of several hundred feet. Since everything in America is measured by football fields, the distance bore some relationship to one, but I couldn't say what. I saw car tracks that led into piñons, to a place where a small vehicle would be visible from the road, but just barely. There was only one track, the toy-size tires of the Nissan, but there were a whole lot of footprints, some of which looked like Lonnie's boot, most of which were probably cops screwing up the scene, none of which were Vs. I walked a little farther, didn't see any more tire tracks or any footprints either, turned around and went back to the parking area where there's a barbed-wire fence that circles the ruins. The fence was about waist high and wasn't hard to climb over—sober.

As I climbed over it I remembered a piece of advice I read when I was in law school. I didn't find it in the law library either, but on the trail map of the Pecos Wilderness where I used to hike with a boyfriend in the summer. "Leave only footprints, take only pictures," the map said. "Plan carefully, prepare thoroughly, practice good manners as you travel through the country. Count on no one but yourself." I wondered if Lonnie had been counting on anyone when she came here. Had it been snowing? Had she or they left tracks in it? Today the path was dry and dusty, patterned by the hieroglyphics of Reebok, Adidas and Nike.

I walked past some pink, people-size mounds beside the path, came to a place where footsteps have worn a shoulder-deep trench in the soft rock and squeezed through. It was no place for fat people. The Indians who lived here were a lot smaller, more agile and better adapted to the environment than we are. The stone from here on was soft and gray and when you stepped on it it turned to powder. There were white tracks like ghosts' footsteps all over the cliffs. I followed them and climbed the mesa. Even if there had been no moonlight when Lonnie was here and if she didn't have a flashlight, she could have followed the white tracks.

As I got near the top of the mesa, the only sounds I could hear were my own footsteps, the legs of my pants rubbing together, an occasional squawking bird and the breeze blowing through wind-stunted trees carrying sounds from the past: Indians walking, talking, carrying water and babies, polishing stone, living in harmony. The only records they left were the petroglyphs they scratched in the stone, but it seems like it was a good place to live, the ruins, a place where people were in harmony with the environment and each other. It wasn't a bad place to die either. If that's what Lonnie wanted, it was her body and her right—if.

Once I went to an Indian ceremonial with her at the Puye cliff dwellings several miles down the road. Ceremonials are religious occasions and usually taping and photography are not permitted. At this one tourists were allowed to walk right up and stick microphones and cameras in the faces of the dancers. It seemed like a travesty and we left. Later that afternoon a storm blew up and two Indians on the mesa were struck by lightning and killed. There was a lot of speculation about how a Pueblo Indian would interpret this. The obvious answer was that the gods were angry, but Lonnie thought the people struck by lightning had been chosen.

Somewhere at the top of the mesa where the path winds through the ruins of a flattened pueblo, I lost it. I knew which way to go, over the top of the cliff and down to the caves. If I followed the edge I'd eventually come to the ladder that led down, but it felt a whole lot lonelier with no path to follow. Drunk or drugged as she may have been,

Lonnie had found the place and climbed down, down one of those primitive wooden ladders that lead to nowhere in Georgia O'Keeffe paintings. This one went down to a trail that followed the cliff. It's a narrow path with a sharp drop-off in places. If you fell here, you could break an ankle and wait until a Pete Vigil happened by or exposure got you.

With a dry cottonwood mouth I walked out toward the end of the path, toward the place where the cliff comes to a point and the piñons roll away like waves. There's a deer etched in the stone out here about five feet tall with antlers. Even though it is only a couple of scratches in a soft stone cliff, it has an expression—alert, watchful. In those days there was a relationship between the hunter and the hunted, some point to the killing. Man was still a part of the animal kingdom, a prey as well as a predator.

I looked at the deer, thought my thoughts, and then there was nothing to do but turn around and walk back. The caves were stacked in the cliff to my right like studio apartments with powdery white foot- and handholds leading up. I found the one I wanted and climbed in, wishing I had some water to unstick my mouth. The petroglyph that had made this cave, in Lonnie's mind, a power spot had been scratched on the soot-blackened wall. She called it the water bearer. A stick figure held a pot high and poured water from it. The water ran into a stream that flowed to a river. Lonnie thought it was a symbol of distributing something—peace, knowledge or maybe just water in a place where it was needed. It was an image that had been here at least five hundred years, waiting, pouring.

The cave's sandy floor was covered with footprints, running shoes, hiking boots, no Vs that I saw, although there were some crescents that might have been made by Lonnie's boot heel. A couple of charred logs were in the center of the cave. The spot where Lonnie had lain must have been stepped on again and again, because I couldn't find it. They say a crime scene reflects the personality of the criminal, but here it's just as likely to reflect the personality of the police. You should keep your hands in your pockets at a crime scene, your feet in place, your eyes open, your mind alert. I stood still and thought about what the scene revealed. The killer, if there was a killer, must have been someone Lonnie knew. Even Lonnie wouldn't have come out here with someone she didn't know, although someone might have followed her. That person would have to be what they call an organized killer, one who planned, left few or no marks on the body, and a person who wanted to spend time with their victim. If they came here soon after Lonnie left me the killer had all night and no one within shouting distance. Unless, of course, there was more than one.

Once I'd done all I could without disturbing the scene I got down on my hands and knees and crawled across the floor sifting the sand through my fingers, turning rectangles and octagons into grains. I was looking for something, but not what got caught in my fingers: a gum wrapper, a nickel, a dime, an empty film canister. I smoothed my hand back and forth across the floor, then ran it around the place where the stone and sand met. It touched something that didn't belong there. I brushed the sand away and picked it up with the plastic Baggie I'd taken from Lonnie's kitchen. The object I'd found was a red plastic knob, the kind that is attached to the drawstring of a sleeping bag. I folded the bag over the knob and closed it. As I eased it into my pants pocket, I heard footsteps. I was a woman alone in a lonely place with fear sharpening my perceptions. A long shadow fell across the mouth of the cave and I felt winter all over again. The shadow was followed by a pair of running shoes, jeans, a camera silhouetted against the view.

"Hey, look at this," a man said, once, and then once more as his voice echoed around the cave.

"What?" a woman replied, following him in. "What? What? What?" They were talking about the water bearer, but then they noticed me squatting in the corner.

"What are you doing?" the guy asked.

"I dropped a roll of film." I showed him the canister, wondering if he'd be observant enough to notice I wasn't carrying a camera.

"That white car parked by the road. It must be yours," the guy said. He had been observant enough to notice that.

"Yeah."

"How 'bout that? We got the same rental car."

"They're pretty common."

"That's how we found the ruins, we saw your car. We heard this place was here but we probably *never* would have found it if it wasn't for your car."

"Great."

"Who lived here anyway?" he asked.

"Indians."

"What did they do?"

"Lived, died," I said. "Raised kids . . . walked in beauty."

"What?"

"Nothing. I have to get going." I stood up and tried to shake some blood back into my legs while the two of them argued about which film to put in their camera.

I walked the mile or so to the road, fifteen minutes, maybe, in time; five hundred years in atmosphere. When I got to the parking area I saw the two white Rich Fords parked side by side. I got in mine and drove back down the mesa, squishing the legger's spongy brakes as it drifted around the hairpin curves. When I got to the highway, I turned right and headed for the Cottonwood truck stop in La Luz to have something to eat and see if anyone could tell me where Pete Vigil lived.

Truckers love the Cottonwood—the parking lot is always full of diesels with women's names scrolled across them, not necessarily the same women engraved in tattoos on the drivers' arms. The waitresses are lush, gorgeous, hot-eyed Hispanic girls. One lesson I learned when I lived in Mexico is that Mexican girls can wear skintight clothes, sulk and pout all day long and no one considers them an easy mark or follows them down the street whispering *psst, psst, moneca, little doll,* but any blue-jeaned *gringa* is fair game. Every culture is full of clues; the hard part for the outsider is interpreting them. I parked the legger, went into the Cottonwood, sat down at a plastic booth and ordered a bowl of green chile stew.

"That chile is *hot,*" said my waitress implying, maybe, that I would be better off with tuna on white. Her name, Raquel, was embroidered on her shirt.

"Good," I replied, "that's how I want it."

"Okay." It was a simple, two-syllable word but she made an aria out of it, making me wonder if there might be a place for her down the road at the Santa Fe Opera.

When the stew was ready, Raquel plunked it down on the table. It was hot, the hottest, maybe, I'd ever had and I bet they'd made it even hotter just for me. I've had *caldos* in Mexico that you fish around in with a spoon trying to get ahold of something, anything, that doesn't have a flaming red chile on it, but I searched for the chiles in this stew and piled them on. They were hot, all right, just like she said, tiny green zingers. My eyes watered and tears dropped in the stew but I kept on eating and weeping, until I'd cleaned my bowl. When I finished I wiped my eyes and blew my nose. The performance made me feel better, but if the waitresses were impressed they didn't let it show. Raquel brought the bill over and I asked her if she could tell me where Pete Vigil lived.

"Who wants to know?" she said in a tone that implied tips were of no consequence to her.

"Me."

"Why do you want to see him?"

"Because a friend of mine died at the ruins last weekend and he found the body."

"That *puta.* " She rolled her eyes. The opera she belonged in was a Mexican soap.

"You knew her?" I asked.

"I know her kind," Raquel said.

Maybe *puta* was a synonym for *gringa* here. I could have responded, "Who are you to say my friend was a whore?" but the green chile stew had taken the fight out of me, I was outnumbered, and besides I'm a lawyer not supposed to let emotion overcome judgment. I'm also a woman with a Hispanic lover who doesn't like to believe the two cultures can't find some way to commingle. They say you should never judge anyone until you've walked a mile in their shoes and who knew what insults *gringas* had dumped on Raquel? "So do you know where Vigil lives?" I asked.

"Over there," she waved in a southerly direction. "Across the river. He's got a big dog and a blue-and-white Chevy."

"*Gracias,* " I replied.

"*Por nada,* " she said.

I got back on the highway, passed the Cuyamunga Stone Company Rock Shop and turned right. The radio was tuned to KMIO, K-mio, Espanola, Santa Fe, playing songs of love gone bad full of "*lo sientos*" and "*te quieros.* " I came to a bridge across a fifty-foot-wide riverbed with three inches of water down the middle—it would take some wishful thinking to call it a river.

Raquel hadn't told me which way to turn once I'd crossed the bridge and I had two choices, not three; turning around and going back was not an option I'd consider. If you're lost in a labyrinth, they say, keep turning left, so I did. After about a quarter of a mile I came to a trailer with a blue-and-white Chevy in the driveway and a black-and-white malamute tied to a tree. The trailer wasn't much to look at, but it was shaded by a couple of tall and aged cottonwood trees and it had a spectacular view across the dry river to the mountains turning to sangria in the setting sun. The place was well taken care of: a fruit tree was about to come into bloom, wood was neatly stacked in a pile. The car and dog were well cared for, too. The dog had a large, majestic head. His face was white with a black mask. His ears picked up but he didn't yap, wag his tail, stand up or make a fuss when he saw me. He was a very calm dog, a breed that was probably not inbred or popular enough to have picked up nervous habits. The car was a two-tone Chevy from the fifties with lots of chrome in immaculate condition. I stood by the door for a minute admiring it.

Pete Vigil came out of the trailer tapping the ground with a stick he used as a cane. He was a small, bowlegged old man with white hair and a mustache to match. He had a kind of rolling cowboy walk pulling himself along with the cane. When he reached the Chevy he asked me in musical English, "You wanna swap?"

"It's a great-looking car," I answered.

"I've had it for thirty years."

"How many miles you got on it?"

"Fifty-three thousand. I only use it to go to the store. You got air conditioning in that one?" He pointed to the legger.

"Yup."

"A radio? Automatic transmission?"

"That, too."

"It's a deal." He shook my hand and smiled. "They call me Pete Vigil."

"Neil Hamel." I smiled back.

"That's my dog. His name is El Rey de los Machos, but

I call him King for short. I wouldn't swap him for any-body."

"I wouldn't either. He's a beauty." King watched us calmly, acknowledging his worth. Pete Vigil seemed to be a man who took care of what was his.

"What can I do you for?" he asked.

"I'm a friend of Lonnie Darmer, the woman you found at the ruins."

"She was your friend?" He shook his head sadly. "I'm very sorry for you. You want to come inside for something to drink?"

"Okay." I followed him into the trailer to his neat and tiny kitchen. He opened the refrigerator, took out two pink plastic bears and poured us some juice.

"Me and King go for a walk every morning," he said. "King don't get excited much, but he smelled something wrong and he took me to your friend. She was dead, you know, when we got there. She looked like a little girl sleep-ing curled up but she was dead."

"Was she in a sleeping bag?"

"No, only her coat, thrown over her like she was trying to keep warm. The fire had gone out."

"Was there anything under her head for a pillow?"

"No, it was on the sand."

"Did you see any footprints?"

"Everywhere. The ruins are full of footprints."

Especially after the police got there, I thought. "The police say it was suicide, but I was with her that night. I can't believe that."

"You wouldn't want to believe it, if you were her friend."

"Did you see anything wrong, any sign that someone else had been there?"

"No, I didn't see anything. She looked very peaceful.

How could somebody have killed her when she wasn't bleeding or hurt?"

"I don't know."

"I'm sorry for you and for her family. It's very, very sad to lose a child or a friend. I know because I lost my boy in Vietnam, and it was the saddest thing that happened to me ever. I'll show you." He went into a tiny bedroom and came back with a picture of his son, a boy in a marine uniform, part Indian, part Hispanic, with straight black hair, liquid brown eyes and cheeks that had been tinted rosy pink in the photograph. He was beautiful enough to make you cry, even if you didn't know he was dead.

"I'm sorry," I said hoping it wasn't tragedy that had made Pete Vigil so kind.

He lifted a pink bear. "Some more juice?"

"No thanks." I pulled out one of my cards and gave it to him. "Would you call me if you think of anything?"

"I sure will." He looked at the card, HAMEL AND HARRISON, it said, LAW OFFICES. "A lawyer?"

"Yes."

"That's a good thing to be. If me and King think of anything, I will call you."

"Thanks a lot."

"It's nothing," he said.

6

The Sangre de Cristo Mountains which frame Santa Fe turn sangria pink at sunset. Albuquerque lies at the base of the Sandias, gray hulks of mountains that look like resting elephants to me. While I drove to work the next morning I thought about the differences between the two places. I do that after I've been north, maybe because somebody always says "Albuquerque? Why would anybody want to live there?" Santa Fe is sixty miles away, two thousand feet higher, three hundred thousand people smaller, and the difference is greater than any of these. It's the difference between historic preservation boards and urban sprawl, the walled in and the wide open, second homes and the homeless, the rich and the middle class. The closest thing Albuquerque has to the City Different is its historic district, Old Town, which has an Adobe of God, narrow streets and the kind of tourist shops they call galleries in Santa Fe. Except for Old Town, Albuquerque is a grid with parallel and perpendicular streets named after the numbers, the states, the elements—Silver, Gold, Copper and Lead, where my law office is located.

It's a place of fast-food chains and strip development, a place where you find Big O Tires, Octopus Car Wash, Desert Treasures Indian Jewelry, Checker Auto Parts, Safeway, Furrs Cafeteria, Custom Hitches U-Haul Rentals, Weinerschnitzel, 7-11, Fat Humphrey's Sub Sandwiches, Soupski at Schlotsky's, Burger King, Pizza Hut, and Wendy's Old Fashioned Hamburgers in a couple of city blocks. We know something about ugly in Albuquerque, but there are times as the sun sets or rises that it lights on a gas station or wall and transforms Lead to gold. A legend that lured the greedy conquistadors ever deeper into New Mexico was the Seven Cities of Cibola, supposedly made of gold. It may have been flecks of straw in the adobe that were illuminated by the rising or waning light, but at the right time of day any city in New Mexico turns golden. The gaudy and cheap appear ugly in old Santa Fe, but here, driving to work early or coming home late, the tacky can be inspiring. A red stoplight is dazzling against the orange sky, plastic flowers are brighter than real and neon shimmers in the sunset.

It was midmorning, however, when I got to my office and Lead was lead. Anna and Brink had already finished breakfast and were wondering what to do next. She handed me a message saying Bunny Darmer had called from a Motel 6.

"Darmer?" said Anna. "Why is that name familiar?"

"Lonnie Darmer was a friend of mine," I answered.

"What do you mean . . . was?" asked Brink. I had forgotten that he'd made moves on Lonnie during one of the off times from Rick. She had been depressed, but not *that* depressed.

"Wait a minute," said Anna. "I know where I heard the

name. Wasn't that the woman who died last weekend near Santa Fe?"

"Yes."

"Lonnie's dead?" asked Brink.

"That city is not safe." That came from Anna, who thought a lot about the subject. She was at the dangerous age, between fifteen and twenty-eight, when 73 percent of the crimes against women are committed, and most of them are committed by men the victims know: lovers, husbands, ex-lovers, ex-husbands. Only 9 percent of known murderers of women are strangers, although those kinds of crimes are on the rise. I get these statistics from FBI studies; they are numbers I remember. Anna continued, "The police called it a suicide, right? Ha! Do you remember the story about the guy in Taos whose head was found in one room and his body in another? They said that was a suicide, too. It pisses me off. How many girls my age have disappeared in Santa Fe in the last few years? Five? Six? And every time it happens the police say 'A twenty-year-old girl disappears, that's no crime.' Then a year later somebody's dog shows up with the skull in its mouth."

"What happened?" Brink asked. Apparently he hadn't watched TV or read a paper this week.

"Lonnie was found dead in a cave at the ruins Sunday morning. She'd been drinking and taking Valium," I told him.

Anna swiveled her chair away from her typewriter. She was sitting with her black nylon legs crossed, tapping a spike-heeled, pointy-toed shoe against the desk. Anna was one person you'd never see in running shoes. There was an advantage to the spike heels she wore; they kept her out of places it was wiser not to go. She was of a generation that didn't feel the need to take risks and explore dark alleys, one that had gone back to the basic American values of comfort and greed. "They're saying she went out to that place alone at night? Forget it. What girl in her right mind would do that?"

"A woman who wanted to die, according to the police," I replied.

"If she wanted to die, she could have done it in her own bed," Anna said. Her generation didn't go out in the wilderness to meditate either.

"Not really, because I spent the night at her place after my car broke down."

"You were with her? Was something wrong?" Brink's eyes were filling up.

"Rick was getting married. She was upset about that."

"If she wanted to be alone, she could have gone to a motel," said Anna.

"Maybe she didn't have the money," Brink said.

"She could have charged it. What difference would it make if she were going to kill herself anyway? Girls don't go into lonely places alone to die. Men take them there to kill them."

"How old was she?" asked Brink.

"Thirty-three."

"So young," he sighed.

I thought so, too, but it probably wasn't so young to Anna. The phone rang. Before she answered it, she told me, "I hope those cops don't get away with this."

The Darmers' Motel 6 was on University in the shadow of I-25 where trucks roared through all night long; not a place anybody stayed for more than one night. When Bunny answered the door it became obvious why she'd insisted on meeting me there and not at my office. She hadn't gotten dressed yet and looked like she might never get dressed again. She was wearing a flannel nightgown, flip-flops and an old plaid bathrobe, the same bathrobe, maybe, whose shoulders Lonnie's head had rested on as a baby thirty-three years ago, the same bathrobe she put on every morning for cornflakes and coffee with Arthur, the same bathrobe in which she was likely to die. I could see her getting into a compact car with Arthur wearing that same bathrobe and driving back home to Roswell. I could see her sitting in that house in Roswell, smoking menthol cigarettes, watching soap operas every day, wearing that bathrobe. She'd let her hair go gray and forget to wash and set it. There were already silver roots at the edge of the gold. She hadn't bothered to put on any new makeup or wash off yesterday's, and there were black streaks of mascara shadowing her eyes.

She let me in to their room (vintage Motel 6) and motioned me to a chair. She and Arthur sat down on the bed. There was a wrought-iron chandelier over a phony wooden table, brown wall-to-wall carpeting and white fake stucco walls. The curtains were drawn, the TV was on but the sound and color weren't and a gray horizontal pattern flickered across the screen like a transmission from *Voyager II*, a galaxy away.

"Bunny's not feeling well," Arthur said, patting her hand, which lay between them on the tacky motel spread. He didn't look so good himself; his eyes had a glazed stare, his cheeks were caving in and his chin was sprouting gray and white stubble.

"Let me be, Arthur." Bunny took her hand back and opened a manila envelope that lay on the bed. "I want to show you something, Neil. This is a copy of the Office of Medical Investigations report they gave us."

It said pretty much what I had expected, that the most probable time of death was in the early morning hours of March 18. The only signs of trauma on the deceased's body were the bruises that could have been caused by rough consensual sex. No defense wounds, no scratches, no needle marks. Her blood alcohol level was high and there was a significant amount of Valium in her system. Not enough of either to have killed her separately, but in combination they could have. The body was covered with a down coat, she was lying beside the ashes of a fire, there was no evidence of hypothermia. The deceased had a history of alcohol and substance abuse, she had been despondent over the breakup of a relationship, she had been seen drinking heavily earlier in the evening, there was an empty container of Valium in her pocket.

"What do you think?" Bunny asked me.

"I don't know," I replied.

"You were with my baby the night she died, weren't you?"

"Yes."

"Tell us what happened," Arthur asked, patting Bunny's hand again.

I told them. When I got to the part about Lonnie crying over Rick, Arthur snapped, "She'd be alive today if it wasn't for that lousy SOB."

"Be quiet, Arthur," Bunny said, but this time she let his hand rest on top of hers on the motel spread: his was thin with brown liver spots and blue veins tunneling under the skin. Hers was plump, white, hand-lotion soft, and wore a microscopic diamond in a narrow gold ring. I continued my story and when I had finished Bunny asked me if I thought Lonnie had acted like she wanted to kill herself.

"Not really," I said, "but it could have been an accident. Maybe she went out there to meditate, got upset or frightened, took one too many Valiums."

"I don't believe that either," said Bunny.

"There were no marks on the body that could have caused her death."

"They didn't look hard enough," Bunny answered. "My baby didn't have rough consensual sex. Somebody raped her."

"There are a few things that bother me," I told her. "One is, Who cleaned up before the wake?"

"Bunny," Arthur said. "She always cleans when something goes wrong."

"I stayed up all night Sunday cleaning. I couldn't sleep," Bunny said.

"Did you take the journal?" I asked.

"What journal?" replied Arthur.

"The journal that was in the bedside table."

"No," said Bunny. "There wasn't any journal there on Sunday. Somebody stole it, I bet."

"There's another thing." I took the red sleeping-bag knob encased in plastic from my purse and showed it to them.

"What's that?" asked Arthur.

"I think it's the knob that goes on the tie to a sleeping bag. I went out to the cave at the ruins to see what I could find and this is it."

"You went out *there?*" Bunny shivered, pulling her robe tight. "I could never go to that place myself."

It's what lawyers do—all the miserable things people can't or won't do for themselves. "For a while I thought you might want to see her ashes scattered there."

"Never. My daughter will be buried in a cemetery in Roswell where she belongs. If she'd stayed home, she'd be alive today."

"Her sleeping bag was in the car Saturday night," I said. "It wasn't there at the wake. Did either of you take it or put it in the trunk?"

"There wasn't any sleeping bag in the car when we got it," Bunny said, "just an old blanket."

"The cops probably stole it," Arthur said.

"It's always a possibility," I replied.

Bunny sat up straighter and pulled her robe tighter. "I'll tell you one thing, my daughter did *not* commit suicide, no matter what this . . . this report . . ." She shook the manila envelope. ". . . Or the police say. She was murdered, and we are going to prove it."

With what? I wondered. There were no witnesses who'd come forward. The evidence we didn't have could fill a black hole, the evidence we might have rattled around in the palm of my hand. As Bunny straightened up and stared at me with faded blue eyes shadowed by grief and mascara but fierce with determination, I saw a woman who would get dressed again, who would wash and dye her hair, a woman who would hire a lawyer to go to the police station and demand that her daughter's death be investigated, go to the district attorney if the police didn't respond, and to the attorney general if the DA didn't respond. If the case ever came to trial this woman would take an active part in the prosecution. She'd listen to every word of testimony if she were admitted to the courtroom, and spend every minute outside the courtroom door if she were not. This was a woman whose fierce desire to see that justice was served would give her strength and could actually bring her to the moment when her daughter's killer was convicted. The convicted might get a life sentence, might cop a plea and get only fifteen, might be a juvenile and be sentenced to a couple of years at the school in Springer. It would put a period at the end of the paragraph, but it would never be enough, would never bring her daughter back, and what then? Would she go back to Roswell and get into her plaid bathrobe all over again?

Bunny watched me with her runny blue steely eyes. "Will you represent us?" she asked me.

"Yes," I said.

After I left them I drove over to the County Court to file some papers and parked the legger in the underground parking lot. When you leave the brilliant sunshine of New

Mexico, it takes a blind moment for your eyes to adjust to the dark. I didn't feel like going back to the office yet so I took a walk after I filed the papers. Downtown is not a neighborhood lawyers like to walk in, even if they do conduct their business here. They may sit in the sunshine of Civic Plaza and eat their lunch, but afterwards they get back to work. The people who hang out downtown—and maybe even live here—are the guys with bedrolls in Crossroads Park, which fronts on Central, the old Route 66, the road hobos once hitchhiked across the country on, looking for jobs. We don't have hobos anymore, we don't even have bums, we have the homeless, but it seems to me there was a time when we didn't have any of these. The ranks of the homeless have increased exponentially in Albuquerque and a lot of other places thanks to the Reagan administration. Someday people will look back on the Reagan years as the big nap without the responsibility. While the administration dozed and stole, the nation's infrastructure collapsed.

I stop by Crossroads Park now and then just to stay in touch. The guys with the bedrolls are, in at least one sense, my peers. They seem to be about the same age—middle to late thirties —although maybe a little worse for wear; sleeping outside takes its toll. They look like Vietnam vets, but who knows whether they are—it's their age, the long hair, the camouflage clothes, and something wounded but kind of gallant about them. Just like the women who take their pillows to seminars in Santa Fe, they carry their bedding with them, rolled up under their arms, children of God, seekers after something, even if it's only a place to lie down. I bought an iced tea to go at The Stuffed Croissant and, as I walked through the park, one of the guys hit me up for thirty-six cents. "Just thirty-six cents," he said, as if being specific meant he wasn't begging. I didn't begrudge him the thirty-six cents, but I didn't want to stand there, holding my iced tea in one hand, fishing through my purse for the money with the other, so I kept on going.

I turned down Central and got stuck behind a fat guy in a T-shirt wearing a large tattoo of a heart pierced by an arrow on his arm. He was too slow to follow, but too fat to pass. You lose your maneuvering skills when you don't walk much. At the library a bunch of guys hung around waiting for a bus, smoking joints. A man sat on the curb wearing a white suit and dark blue glasses that reflected the Kimo Theatre and maybe even myself. One of my colleagues was about to open an office in the black glass building at 500 Marquette Street, so I went over there to take a look. There were huge ficus trees, a mass of greenery behind the glass, and when I got into the lobby and tried to read the black glass directory, all I could see was the reflection of the trees. There was a time when visual distortions seemed to sharpen one's perceptions, but these reflections made it impossible for me to find the guy's name.

Before I got back into my car and drove the five blocks to my office like a true American, I sat in the wide open spaces of Civic Plaza for a few minutes. There weren't many of us here; all the courthouse staff had finished lunch and gone back to work. Only the unemployed and the self-employed like me take time off in the middle of the afternoon. My excuse was that, like visual distortions, breaking habits can help you to see. The purple petunias were blooming in their concrete containers. A homeless person poked through a garbage bin looking for his share of somebody else's lunch. I sat on a bench under a massive concrete pavilion that made pagodalike shadows on the ground, watched a girl in a red T-shirt run through the plaza and thought about what you notice as a person approaches. First would probably be the color the person wore, then the person's general shape and size, sex, age, attractiveness or lack of same, how the person is dressed, what that reveals about them, all the obvious. Then there was the other side, the side you don't usually look at that might reveal something else. I began watching the shadows of the people who walked across the plaza. With the clear air and the ever-present sun, shadows are prominent here. First I saw a fat, round cloud follow an ebullient woman, and then two thin shadows, about the same length, walking in unison step for step, shadowing each other. The old couple they followed were in sync, too.

My thoughts led to Lonnie, as all thoughts tended to these days. The police and the medical director were looking at this case in the way they had gotten accustomed to seeing a case, examining the obvious. But maybe there was something that couldn't be seen, something not evident but implied, something conspicuous by its absence. I remembered a man named Robert Fitch who I met at Bailey's, the singles bar where the young professionals hang out, a few years ago. He had been a paramedic and a medical investigator. He'd called me several times for dates, but I'd always turned him down. I got my car out of the underground garage, went back to my office and gave him a call. It was a few minutes before he remembered who I was. "Neil Hamel," I said, "remember? We dated a couple of times a few years ago?" It was an exaggeration but it did the trick. I asked if I could buy him a drink after work.

"As it happens, I'm free," he said.

7

I met him at Bailey's on Louisiana, filled with potted plants and uprooted people and about as crowded at this time of day as a Mexican bus. It was a good place to have a private conversation because everybody else was too busy scoring to listen. Robert Fitch was dressed in hiking boots and the kind of boring outdoor clothes you get in army-navy stores. His hair fell across his forehead in lopsided bangs that told me he'd cut it himself. He was tall and thin with the look of a large, awkward and solitary bird. He stood up and his arms flapped when he saw me.

"Neil," he said, "how have you been?" He bent over to give me a peck.

"Good," I replied, kissing the air near his left cheek.

He'd gotten there before me and I was happy to see he had been able to find us a booth; I think better sitting down. Robert had a German beer sitting in front of him, and I ordered a margarita from a waitress I didn't know. Sally, my favorite bartender, didn't work here anymore. She'd had a brief relationship with Brink and shortly thereafter moved to California, probably to get away from him.

"So how's the medical investigator business?" I asked Robert for openers.

"I got out of it."

"You did?"

"I'm out of the paramed business, too. I always wanted to be a writer, you know."

I didn't, although I probably should have. Scratch the surface of most people in northern New Mexico and you find an aspiring something. "What kind of writing do you do?"

"Well, I used to write mysteries, and I thought doing medical investigations would give me ideas." Medical investigators come from all walks of life in New Mexico: funeral directors, paramedics, writers. Only the medical director has to be a doctor.

"Did they?" My margarita arrived heavily encrusted with salt.

"I learned a lot, but it was depressing getting up in the middle of the night to look at the remains of people who had self-destructed or been wiped out by someone else. It was bad enough to be doing it, I found I didn't want to be writing about it afterwards."

I licked my way through the barrier reef of salt, arrived at a sheltered cove of triple sec and tequila, took a sip. "So what are you doing now?"

"Technical writing, computer manuals, that sort of thing."

"You like it?"

"Actually, I do. It's a steady source of income, the work is challenging, I enjoy working with computers. I'm thinking about moving up to Los Alamos. That's where most of the work is." I could see it. He had the lack of concern for physical appearance that was typical of Los Alamoseños, the kind of lost-in-the-stars, interested-in-the-way-things-work, uninterested-in-what-I-wear look. The kind of guy who would pay $500 over the sticker price for a Toyota because he liked the engineering and spend $25 a year on clothes. He had a mind that was good at detail and facts, the mind of a technical writer, not a novelist, but that was okay with me; it was detail that I was after.

"Would you mind if I picked your brain a bit?" I asked.

"Not at all." He leaned forward eagerly, knocking over what little beer was left in his glass. "Oops, sorry," he said. I helped him wipe it up with paper napkins.

"I'll get you another." I flagged down the waitress.

"I'll get it."

"No, it's on me. I could use your help."

"What's the problem?"

"I'm representing the family whose daughter was found dead at the ruins last weekend."

"Oh, yeah, I read about that one. Suicidal or accidental combination of drugs and alcohol, right?"

"That's what the medical director said. The parents don't want to believe it."

"Well they wouldn't, would they?"

"No, but the other alternative's murder. Is that any better?"

"In a way; it absolves them of responsibility. If a daughter is depressed or careless enough to kill herself, it doesn't say much for the parents, does it?"

It didn't say a whole lot for the friends either.

"Have you seen the medical director's report?" Robert asked me.

"Yeah, and I've got a copy of it here if you'd like to take a look."

His beer arrived and I paid for it while he looked at the report. "Alcohol and Valium in her system, although not all that much. Ordinarily it takes a lot of Valium to kill someone, but if she took it all at once mixed with alcohol, who knows? Everybody's different. It's not the best drug to commit suicide with because it does take so much. You're more likely to end up in a coma than dead, but maybe she didn't know that. It's a drug you build up a tolerance for, too. Had she been taking it for a long time?"

"Long as I've known her."

He continued studying the report. "No signs of hypothermia, no defense wounds, no scratches, no needle marks, only some bruises that were probably caused by consensual sex."

"How do they know the bruises were caused by consensual sex? Couldn't she have been raped?"

"Maybe. A medical director couldn't necessarily tell."

"Since they made a determination that drugs and alcohol killed her, couldn't they have been more specific?"

"Not necessarily. Autopsies are not an exact science, especially when it comes to drugs and they're acting in synergy. The mere presence of a substance doesn't mean it killed someone either. It's not like you can zip a body open and find a marker that says this is what caused the death. A good medical director has to consider more than physical evidence. Witnesses can help, if you have any. You also have to consider history and circumstances. Apparently she was a despondent substance abuser who was alone when she died."

"Who knows whether she was alone? Police aren't always noted for their attention to detail at crime scenes."

"That's true." He gave the report back to me. "The police are not supposed to touch the body or move anything until we get there, but more often than not they do. That's another reason I don't do medical examinations anymore—the lack of cooperation from the police. Every case of sudden death should be considered a homicide and investigated as such, but they aren't necessarily. Who's in charge of the investigation?"

"There isn't any investigation, but the person who should be in charge is Michael Railback."

"Oh, him. He's a stubborn shit. Once he makes up his mind, you'll have a hard time convincing *him* to change it."

"Believe me, I know."

Robert sipped at his beer, I licked more salt off the rim of my glass.

"There's one thing you should consider, Neil, parents are never happy with a determination made about a child's death. It's just too awful to face, so they blame the police, the medical investigator, anyone but themselves."

"Lonnie Darmer was also a friend of mine, Robert. I was with her the night she died."

"So you can't let go of it either."

"No. Just for the hell of it suppose she wasn't alone at the ruins. Is there any way she could have been murdered without leaving a mark on the body?"

"Actually, there are a couple, but they're rare around here; murderers in New Mexico tend to leave a mark. I suppose someone could have mashed up the Valium, dissolved it in a drink and given it to her, but if they really wanted to kill her, why didn't they give her more?"

"Maybe they gave her all there was. An empty pill container was found at the scene."

"There's suffocation, although that would require a certain passivity from the victim. If you smothered somebody in their sleep, say, and the victim didn't struggle, there might not be any marks. Of course, there could be saliva, hairs, makeup, etcetera, on the pillow or whatever was used to smother, but you'd have to find it first."

"How about a sleeping bag?"

"That could do it. You can also kill someone by compressing the carotid arteries and cutting off the supply of blood to the brain." He put his fingers to his throat to show me where the arteries were. "Again, if the victim didn't struggle, there might not be bruises. Compressing the artery and cutting off the blood supply to the brain causes dizziness and blacking out. Supposedly it intensifies orgasm; it also incapacitates a victim. Lovers do it to their partners, and rapists to their victims—they call it the carotid sleeper. *Carotid*, incidentally, comes from the Greek word *karos*, meaning heavy sleep. It's a dangerous practice; seconds of blood deprivation to the brain can be fatal."

"Could that produce hallucinations or visions if it didn't cause death?"

"God knows. A heightened awareness anyway. There's something teenagers do—pulling against a rope or a scarf around their neck while they are masturbating—that can result in death. It's called autoerotic asphyxia. I don't know if the thrill comes from oxygen deprivation or blood deprivation or both. It must be intense for anyone to take the risk. Of course, in that case there would be rope burns. There's cartilage in the neck that doesn't become bone until a person is in their forties or fifties. In an older person pressure on the neck might result in broken bone, but in a younger person it wouldn't. In some cases of strangulation, but not all, you see petechiae, pinpoint hemorrhaging on the lining of the eyelids. Anyway, to answer your question, yes, there are ways a person could be murdered with no marks on the body, but it would take a passive or trusting victim. Given the facts of this case, I probably would have made the same determination the medical director did. Unless you can find a murder weapon or a witness or get a confession, you're going to have a hard time proving otherwise. I'll give you some criminal profile tips, however, that might help. Stranger murder is on the rise, but most murderers know their victims and sex murderers are usually the same race and around the same age as their victims.

A lot of these guys are stalkers and it's the chase that turns them on. Sexual agression isn't always evidenced at the crime scene, and the victims aren't necessarily raped. Some of these guys masturbate over the victim after she's dead."

I leaned over to take a look at a clock hidden behind a large spider plant. The subject had a certain morbid fascination, but I had an appointment at home and I'd learned what I needed to. "Many thanks, Robert, you've been a big help," I said. "If I can ever return the favor, give you advice about the law, say, I'd be happy to."

"I'll let you know." He flapped his arms in preparation for flight. "What are you doing for dinner?" he asked.

"I'm seeing someone now. He's coming over."

"Just my luck," Robert said.

I would have told the Kid about Lonnie eventually. In fact, I intended to the very next time I saw him, but Anna did it first when he called the office while I was out. Anna neglected to tell me that she had told him, however, and he surprised me by showing up with a six-pack of Tecate, a bag full of tacos and a red rose in a jar. The rose floated in some kind of pickling solution that would keep it velvety and red for eternity.

"Kid, you shouldn't have!" I said.

"I'm sorry about your friend, Chiquita." He handed me the rose.

"Thanks." I gave him a kiss.

"The live flowers smell good but in a couple of days they're dead." He shrugged. "This one will last forever."

"You're right."

The obvious place for the rose was the mantel, over a fireplace that got used about once a year when some guy showed up at the doorway with an armload of piñon to sell. Piñon smells good but burns fast, and most of the aroma goes up the chimney in smoke. Since the fireplace was used so seldom, the mantel had become a catchall for keys, gloves and *objets d'art*. There was a picture of a white bird against a blue sky, various candles and candlesticks, an arrangement of dried flowers, a photograph of the Kid and two white cow vertebrae that I found years ago while hiking in the Pecos Wilderness. The vertebrae looked like flying zeros, circles surrounded by wings of bone, wings that start out as cartilage but end up as bone. Georgia O'Keeffe said that when she came to New Mexico she picked bones because she couldn't find any flowers, but now I had both, flowers and bones that would last forever. I placed the pickled rose right smack in the middle of the mantel. "It's beautiful, Kid," I told him. "Thanks a lot."

"It's nothing, Chiquita," he said.

8

The next day was Thursday, the day of Rick's party and the day I get to watch "L.A. Law" if I arrive home on time, a day on which I went to see Detective Railback once again. He was ready for me, sitting at his desk playing with a paper clip. I sat myself down and handed him the sleeping bag knob in its plastic Baggie. "I found this in the cave where Lonnie Darmer died," I said.

"What is it?"

"The knob from a sleeping bag."

"How do you know that?"

"Because I've seen them attached to sleeping bags."

He shrugged, laid the bag on his desk. Police are not always known for the care with which they store evidence, either.

"If you don't believe me, go downtown to Climb High and take a look at their bags," I said.

"How do you know it came from *her* sleeping bag?"

"I don't, but her sleeping bag was missing, and I found this a few feet from where she died."

"When?"

"Tuesday."

"Lonnie Darmer died Sunday morning."

"It's not like a whole lot of people are going to break into the ruins and sleep in a cave where a woman has just died suspiciously."

"We went over that cave with a fine-tooth comb."

An Afro pick would be more like it.

"And what was suspicious about her death anyway?" Railback asked. "She killed herself." He squeezed the paper clip and it sprung from his fingers, pinging as it hit the desk.

"A former medical investigator told me it was unlikely anyone would try to kill themselves with Valium. Someone could have dissolved it in a drink and given it to her. It would also be possible to smother a person or compress the carotid arteries and cut off the blood supply to the brain without leaving any bruises or marks, he said."

"Who told you that?"

"Robert Fitch."

"That sounds like Fitch. That guy thinks he's some kind of crime expert. Just for the record, the crime lab examined your friend's clothes and the coat she was wearing and they didn't find any blood, semen or saliva, no hairs but hers and some cats', no fingerprints but her own, no evidence, no crime."

"You didn't examine the sleeping bag."

"You're the only one says there was a sleeping bag. You mind telling me what your interest is in all this?"

"The Darmers hired me to represent them. They're concerned that there's been no investigation of their daughter's death."

"Maybe it'll make 'em feel better to blame me, but I

didn't kill her. I can't bring her back neither. Their daughter did it to herself, plain and simple. They might as well face it and the sooner the better."

"There is something else that bothers them. Lonnie's journal was missing from her drawer."

"Well, I'm no psychic, but from what I heard about the way that girl lived, she had plenty of reasons to get rid of any record she kept."

"It was there the night she died."

"Who saw it?"

"Me."

Railback lifted his palms and shrugged, as if to imply that was one more piece of evidence that only I saw. "Is that it?"

"For the moment." Nature's law of bureaucratic inertia is that whenever one of our elected or appointed officials takes a position it gets engraved on his or her stony heart, and Railback's was as stony as anyone's. Like Robert said, he was a stubborn shit. Well, he wasn't the only person I knew in Santa Fe County law enforcement. I happened to have gone to law school at UNM with Dennis Quinlan, who was now the district attorney. I stood up, pulled my shades down and got ready to leave.

"Your Ray-Bans are crooked again," Railback said.

My next stop was Rick's party. I drove downtown to First Associates' office, which was in a low-slung territorial building with a long portal in front and Santa Fe blue trim on the windows and doors. Either Rick's taste had improved or Marci Coyle had picked the spot. It gave me hope that the Ugly Building wouldn't be so bad after all; maybe Lonnie had let emotion get in the way of judgment. I remembered an office Rick once built himself in nearby Madrid that was made out of metal and shaped like a snail on end. It made a statement, but you couldn't stand up straight on the curly floors, the metal rusted and the skylights leaked on your head. It was built during Rick's experimental extended-sixties period, in a New Mexico mountain town where the sixties will never die. Obviously, no historic preservation board would ever approve that. They could be tough in Santa Fe. I attended a hearing for a client a few years ago when a man (not my client, thank God) was trying to get permission to paint his window sills lilac. Trim had to be in natural colors, the Historic Preservation Board said; lilac did not qualify. The man showed up at the meeting in a purple shirt carrying a bunch of lilacs and a jar full of lilac-colored sand. The HPB was not amused, the lilac was not approved.

Rick's office being in downtown Santa Fe, there was no place to park and I had to drive five blocks farther before I found a space. The car in the spot ahead of me had Santa Fe plates and a bumper sticker that said FUCK OFF AND DIE, one native, maybe, who had seen too many tourists. I walked back and as I turned the corner I heard the chant, "Ugly, ugly, ugly." While I parked a number of demonstrators had materialized in front of Rick's office wearing ugly masks: Jim and Tammy Bakker, Ron and Nancy Reagan, Leona Helmsley, Donald Trump, Richard Nixon. Greedy people and ugly, too. The demonstrators carried signs that said STOP THE UGLY and WHO GOT $NUGGLY WITH UGLY? It was good to know that demonstrations were still alive and well. Lonnie would have been proud of them. She would have been one of them.

The uglies annoyed the guests, but they didn't keep anyone from going inside. Santa Fe society, in their best turquoise and silver jewelry, crossed the ugly line. I hesitate to cross a picket line myself, and I stood at the edge of the portal, obviously not one of Santa Fe's best, wondering what to do next. Richard Nixon came up, offered me his arm and escorted me to the door. "Thanks, Dick," I said. He nodded his large, rubber elephant-man head and his oversized jowls shook. "Stop the Ugly," he mumbled in a voice heavily muffled by the mask.

Once inside I made my way to the bar, where they were serving fruit, cheese and champagne. I helped myself to a glass, took a chocolate-covered strawberry and began circling the party, working my way slowly from the perimeter to the center where the model was located, keeping an eye out for Rick and wondering which of the women present was the shark-faced Marci Coyle. There were a lot of architects around talking architect talk.

"I've made a conscious decision to stay inside the perimeter and manipulate the existing space." That came from an elegant, silver-haired guy in a blazer.

"I can understand it. A new building is a blank slate, but renovation, now *there's* a living animal." Spoken by a long-haired cohort in jeans and boots.

"I'm dressing the bones, making no attempt at a statement beyond its own sake, you understand. As an expression of its function, the exterior will have no unnecessary apertures. I'm interested in the effect of the variant upon the mass obtained by popping out the kitchen window. The irregular symmetry of the courtyard will prepare you for the rest of the house. As you enter things become less geometric, more fluid. It may be a game but it works."

"It's the only game in this town."

"That's for sure. I'm making videotapes as we go and sending them to the clients."

"In L.A.?"

"Yeah."

I needed a cigarette after that so I lit up. "Do you mind?" A fit blonde stood next to me nibbling on a slice of kiwi and sipping a designer water. She'd probably played three sets of tennis, run round the track and been to an aerobics class already today.

"Mind what?" I asked.

"Not smoking. This is a smoke-free environment."

"It is? I thought it was a party."

"Please," she replied, waving her hand in front of her nose.

I took a few more drags and looked for a place to put out my maligned Marlboro. As there were no ashtrays I was forced to fertilize a ficus tree. Eventually I made my way to Rick, who was standing beside the table that supported the model. It took a large chunk out of the center of the room. There were a lot of things wrong with the First Building; proportion was one of them, the Penitentiary Modern style was another. It did make one wonder that the Historic Preservation Board would turn down lilac and approve this. The construction most likely would be cinder block and stucco, but the exterior finish had the rounded look of puddled—or, in this case, muddled—adobe. It works for small, human-scaled buildings and churches, not institutionally inhuman large ones. Rick had striven for monumentality but had created a blob, leaden and massive, with tiny windows spaced high up and evenly like cells. There was a walkway along the top floor and two turrets that would provide good lookouts for guards. The central courtyard was huge and user unfriendly, with wrought-iron grillwork that resembled bars, a perfect place for prisoners to riot or exercise, but no place anyone would want to sit and have a drink or coffee. As Lyndon Baines Johnson once said about his own portrait, it was the ugliest thing I ever saw.

"What do you think?" asked the proud architect.

"I'm a little surprised that the Historic Preservation Board approved it," I replied.

"Why? They know the value of a good project."

"They know the value of something. Well, if anything goes wrong, and your building doesn't get built here, you can always sell the plans to the Texas Department of Corrections."

"You know, that's just about what I've come to expect from you, Neil, a bitter, smart-ass remark."

"And this is just about what I've come to expect from you—stupid, ugly crap."

"Just because your life hasn't turned out the way you wanted . . ." said the newly-successful-and-proud-of-it architect.

"What's wrong with my life?"

"I have to tell you? You have a two-bit law practice for starters, you can't afford a new car or decent clothes and you have a greasy-fingered garage mechanic—a young one—for a lover."

"You want to know something? My greasy-fingered young mechanic knows a hell of a lot more about love than you'll *ever* know. I'm not talking about pursuit or conquest, I'm not talking about technique, I'm talking about love." No doubt everyone in earshot was eavesdropping on this conversation, former lover talk.

"Oh, yeah?" He smiled one of those wide smiles that bared his canines. "How long has it been, anyway, since we, um . . ."

That's the kind of guy who mistakes any interaction between a man and a woman for foreplay. "As far as I'm concerned we didn't," I said.

He put down his champagne glass as if to imply he was through with me. "It's been great seeing you. Why don't we get together again in another fifteen years?"

"I'm not finished yet."

"Now that you've crucified me as a lover and an architect, what's left?"

I lowered my voice. The part of this conversation that might be amusing to an audience was over. "I want to know where Lonnie went the night she died."

"To the ruins," he said.

"I mean before that."

"How the hell should I know? You were the last person to see her alive, weren't you?" He was trying to keep his voice down, but it was a struggle.

"She told me she wanted to see you."

"Yeah?"

"So, where were you that night?"

"Home."

"With Marci?"

"Alone. Marci went back to Texas for the weekend. What's your problem, Neil? You're trying to blame me and Marci when *you're* the one who let Lonnie go off alone and stoned?"

"I didn't let her go. She took off."

"And you couldn't have prevented it? How come I always get the blame for Lonnie? Isn't that what the women's movement is all about—women taking responsibility for themselves? Blame yourself, if you want to, that she's dead, blame her, blame her mother, but leave me out of it." His voice was losing the battle to keep quiet.

"Shh," I whispered, trying to bring the conversation back to a private level. "Maybe she didn't commit suicide."

"You think she was murdered? Someone slid Valium down her throat? Isn't that what you'd like to believe so you don't have to feel any responsibility yourself?"

"Someone could have mashed it up and dissolved it in a drink. Someone could also have compressed the carotid arteries, cut off the supply of blood to her brain, or she could have been smothered and the evidence removed. There would be no marks if she didn't resist."

"Well, if you think she was smothered, you ought to be talking to Ci, not me. That's how she takes people into the next life, you know. She puts a pillow over their face and deprives them of oxygen till they black out and see what's coming."

"That's crazy."

"It's pretty sick, and one more thing that drove Lonnie and me apart. Can I go now? There are other people here I'd like to talk to." He was watching a dark-haired woman in a red suit across the room. Marci Coyle, I figured. She was talking to a guy in a business suit—a prospective tenant, probably—and not paying the least bit of attention to me.

"Go for it," I said.

I went back to the bar, where I got another champagne and a handful of green grapes, and ran into a lawyer I knew from the old days at Lovell, Cruse, Vigil and Roberts. His name was Sandy and he was that kind of guy, sandy hair, ruddy complexion, eager to please. The kind of guy who failed the bar exam three times before he finally passed and got ahead by telling bad jokes. Sandy told me he was going to be transferred to Lovell, Cruse, Vigil and Roberts's Santa Fe office when the Ugly Building opened.

"I guess I'll have to move up here," he said. "It's a bitch of a commute."

"How do you feel about it?" I asked since, considering the relationship between the two cities, moving to Santa Fe was like joining the enemy camp.

"I can handle it." He smiled and his sandy bangs flopped. "They sure take their architecture seriously here. I guess it's the only war in town. Did you see those demonstrators? Whoa!"

"You know, Sandy, there's a lot of opposition to the project. Maybe Lovell, Cruse should think it over. Moving into that building is going to make the firm unpopular here."

"They'll get over it. Carl Roberts feels that the people

who are opposed to the building aren't the people who'll become our clients anyway."

That sounded like something Carl Roberts would think. "A lot of people are surprised the Historic Preservation Board approved it," I said. "You don't happen to know the chairman's name, do you?"

"Jorge Mondragon."

"What does he do in real life?"

"He owns Land of Enchantment Real Estate. He likes the building, but I hear other people are calling it a rape, a rape of Old Santa Fe."

"Something like that."

His grin told me a joke was coming. It was time to move on, but I wasn't fast enough. "Do you know the difference between rape and escape?" he asked.

"No." And I didn't think I wanted to, either.

"With rape you try to prove who's out and gets in, with escape you try to prove who's in and gets out."

"Ha, ha," I said. "I gotta go."

"See ya," he replied.

I didn't think Rick and Marci would spend their time together at this function; they'd want to be circulating. I wandered over to where Marci stood. Rick had gone back to crowing over his model, she'd resumed her conversation with the businessman—something about dollars per square foot and sprinkler systems and tax benefits. She was much too engrossed in the bottom line to notice me watching her. Marci Coyle was small, compact, immaculately dressed in a red suit and high-heeled shoes that cost at least $150 per. She had smooth and shiny brown hair that she probably set in hot rollers on the days she was too busy to get to the hairdresser. Her movements were tense and quick. She wore bright red lipstick, talked fast and, from what I could hear, knew exactly what she was talking about.

9

I made it back to Albuquerque in time to watch "L.A. Law." Victor Sifuentes was representing a small-time Mexican-American brewer who got forced out of business by a rumor (spread by the owner of a large company) that the brewery workers pissed in the beer. The small company sued; the large company hired a token Hispanic lawyer who Victor thought was selling out. As always, Victor was noble, doe-eyed, honest, my favorite character. Anna, however, preferred the sleazy womanizer Arnie Becker.

She wore a purple pouf in her hair the next morning with a miniskirt and lipstick to match. It might be tacky, it might not even be suitable law-office attire, but on her it looked good. She sipped at a Styrofoam cup of coffee and ate something covered with sugary white powder that snowed all over her desk, a jelly doughnut, I guessed. Brink was fat-loading again—greasy sausage and greasy egg on a greasy English muffin, dripping on an already grease-stained suit.

Anna put down her doughnut when she saw me and got tough. "If that means tearing you through the polluted sludge, I'll do it," she snarled in her best Arnie Becker imitation.

"To them you'll never be anything but a spic with a law degree," replied Victor Sifuentes/me.

"Friday morning . . . already?" Brink rolled his eyes up.

As the older and presumably wiser woman in this organization I felt an obligation every Friday to warn Anna about no-good philanderers. "Arnie Becker is a sleazy womanizer in designer shoes," I said.

"He's cute," replied Anna.

"He's a snake."

"He's nice to his secretary, Roxanne," Anna argued. "He gave her a raise, he got her a divorce. He just needs to find the right woman."

"Please. A guy like that won't be happy with any woman and he won't make any woman happy, either."

"He dresses well," said Brink.

"He's a scumbag," I answered. "And Anna, how you can idolize a guy like Arnie Becker and turn around and complain about crimes against women, for God's sake?"

"He's a lover, not a rapist or a murderer."

"Only of the spirit."

"Friday morning . . . again," sighed Brink.

And not that early on Friday morning either. Beginning the day at midmorning was a bad habit. I was a lot more productive when I got up with the sun and drove to work in the flamingo glow, but it didn't happen often. There was already a stack of pink slips waiting for me on Anna's desk, and one of them was from Pete Vigil in La Luz. I would have bet he never watched "L.A. Law." I was wrong, however, because the first thing he asked me when I got him on the phone was if I liked Victor Sifuentes.

"Crazy about him," I said.

"He reminds me of my boy," Pete Vigil replied in his musical English. "I was hoping he would be a lawyer."

"I'd marry Victor tomorrow, if only he'd ask me."

"I was going to ask you to marry me."

"Well, if Victor doesn't come through, I'll think about it. How's King?"

"He's good. How is your investigation going into your friend's death?"

"Not great. The police aren't giving me any help."

"I've been asking around here to see what I can find out."

"Thanks," I said.

"One of my boy's friends who was in Vietnam with him doesn't think it was an accident either."

"Good. When can I talk to him?"

"He will be at the Albuquerque flea market Sunday. Can you come?"

"Yes."

"I'll be there, too. I have some elk antlers to sell. Look for me and I will take you to him."

"Thanks a lot."

"My pleasure," he said.

I took a look through the rest of the pink slips and didn't find anything as pressing or interesting as the next call I had to make—to Dennis Quinlan, my old law-school class-mate and the recently elected Santa Fe County DA. Dennis had followed the straight and narrow path: a wife, two children, a house and a position that required him to be responsible to the community. He was the kind of guy who took his responsibilities seriously, who seemed terminally bland in law school but improved with age. He had taken on a thankless job, although he was doing his best to clean up the mess of unsolved and unprosecuted crimes his predecessor had left. He sounded harried when I got him on the phone.

"Neil, how are you?"

"Not too bad. And you?"

"Overworked. You getting any interesting cases down there?"

"Actually, I've got one in your district."

"Oh, what's that?"

"I'm representing the Darmers, whose daughter died at the ruins last weekend."

"Oh, yeah, the drug overdose, right?"

"The parents don't think so, they think she was murdered."

"Is there any evidence to support that theory?"

"Some. I passed it on to Detective Railback."

"And?"

"Nothing. He's convinced there was no crime."

Dennis sighed. "Well, as you know, it's not really my role to solve crimes, although everybody expects me to. The police are supposed to investigate and bring in someone for me to prosecute."

"I know, Dennis, but the police aren't doing crap and the parents are miserable and angry—with good cause, I think."

"I'd rather not interfere with police investigations, Neil," he said. I knew why: he was relatively new on the job, there had been a lot of conflict between the previous DA and the police, he was trying to develop a better relationship. Implying the police weren't doing their duty was not a good way to get started.

Only the truth was they weren't. "The problem is they're *not* investigating," I said.

Dennis thought it over and I could just about hear the thoughts talking. One of the major problems his predecessor had was an alarming number of unsolved crimes against women: some had been murdered, some had been raped, some had disappeared. Santa Fe has a permanent population of fifty-five thousand, but there are over a million transients and tourists who pass through every year—which was one of the problems, but not the only one. The last thing Dennis needed was a victim's parents complaining loudly and bitterly to the media about the unsolved murder or disappearance of their daughter. He knew it, and so did I.

"You really believe she was murdered?"

"Yes," I said, and gave him my reasons.

"It's not much, Neil."

"It's not so bad considering there hasn't even been an investigation."

"All right, I'll give Railback a call, see if I can light a fire under him."

"Thanks a lot, Dennis."

"You're welcome," he sighed.

That accomplished, I made myself a cup of Red Zinger and took a look at the papers. I didn't find any reference to Lonnie in the *New Mexican*. Among the "Police Notes" I did find this: "A man told police Thursday he jumped from his moving pickup near the corner of Don Gaspar and Paseo de Peralta because he hallucinated that a tree was inside his truck and was trying to grab him."

Next I read the "Journal North" section of the *Albuquerque Journal*. Lonnie had disappeared from this paper, too, an inactive case. Gene Youngblood, a scholar in residence at the College of Santa Fe, had written a column on eroticism in film, which I figured would make a lot more interesting reading than the divorce files on my desk. Although eroticism is often the cause of divorce, what comes afterwards isn't very interesting, at least not to me, even though that's one way I earn my living. What you get is a lot of haggling over possessions and pets and health insurance, some of it valid and necessary, some of it a way of getting back for hurt that was done, and those kinds of hurts can never be compensated for. Now that I've become an expert on divorce my opinion is that lack of sex can hold marriages together and sex can break them up. There's a sort of contract some people make when they feel sexually inadequate or uninspired or whatever. The unwritten contract (and nobody ever puts a contract like that in writing) says, "We'll stay together and nobody else will have to know how inadequate we are." But sooner or later an erotically charged human comes along (there are plenty of them out there) and the contract gets torn apart. And since it was never put in writing and the terms were never clearly stated, it's impossible to enforce.

Gene Youngblood had this to say: "I (am not) denying the beauty and power of sex for its own sake, independent of love, as a kind of transcendent discipline, a path to self-knowledge. The genuine erotomane, like the artist or the revolutionary, is a shaman on the frontiers of consciousness." It was a frontier some of us had been on way back then, the border in the desert across which the invisible globes and colors of choice were found. The edge is an intense place to be and, unless you find the perfect companion, dangerously exposed. You can spend a couple of years there, maybe, but not a lifetime. Most people settle for comfortable sex, or embarrassing sex, or Saturday night sex, or no sex at all. Or you could be like Lonnie, and continue to cross the border leaving your lover behind; I doubted that Rick ever felt the same intensity about the experience that she did, or that he was even capable of it. He was a guy with a lot of technical skills who liked to watch himself at work, one who gave pleasure but didn't feel it, inflicted pain and didn't feel that either. He'd send you across the border—if you let him—and watch from the safe side while you danced alone, exposed in the wind.

I had other things to think about than sex and Rick First, other cases to work on than Lonnie Darmer's—divorces, in fact—but I didn't feel like doing it, so I got out my Santa

Fe phone book and looked up Historic Preservation Board chairman Jorge Mondragon's phone number at Land of Enchantment Real Estate. I asked his secretary if I could see him that afternoon and she said "When?" without any What for? or Who referred you? It's the curse of being a real estate broker, you always have to be available. It's not the only one either—in some circles real estate brokers are despised even more than lawyers—so I had some sympathy for Jorge Mondragon before I met him.

But I may also have been influenced by the Iberian guitar music I heard on the rent-a-Ford radio as I drove the lonesome highway north. Rippling flamenco riffs put me in a Spanish mood; I began thinking about the conquistadors, how they sailed off the edge of the world and ended up in places that looked just like home. They built their most beautiful cities in the high plains, the altiplano, of Mexico, which reminded them of the plains they had left behind in Spain. And they built La Villa Real de Santa Fe de San Francisco de Assisi, a.k.a. Santa Fe, in an area that reminded them of the plains they had left in Mexico.

Jorge Mondragon's office was buried in an ancient complex on Paseo de Peralta. He and the office both had a weary Spanish style, a kind of battered elegance that fit my mood. The suit he wore wasn't expensive, but it was serious. He had silver hair, a thin face, long, white virtuoso's fingers and the rarefied air of an El Greco saint. It was kind of an unusual persona for a real estate broker, but maybe he didn't sell much real estate. No doubt Jorge spoke fluent, maybe even Castilian, Spanish, which would be an asset in his work. I had no trouble getting in to see him; the office was not a hotbed of activity—his secretary filed her nails and the phones barely rang while I was there. On the walls of the reception room there were pictures of him posing with various clients, some Hispanic, some not, a few well known, most not. His secretary told me to go right on into his office so I did. It had a cool, damp, mushroomy feeling and the look of a room in the depths of a colonial home where the sun doesn't dare shine. You have to be buried deep in New Mexico to find that. The light was artificial, the walls white, the furniture massive and dark. There was wrought-iron grillwork on the lone window and in the corner a bookcase full of photographs. It looked more like a shrine than a home for books. I got the feeling that before Jorge Mondragon left at night he pulled white candles and flowers out of his desk drawer, lit the candles, floated the flowers in water and placed them before the photographs. They were all of a woman, about forty I'd say, making her fifteen to twenty years younger than him. She had semi-bouffant, sprayed-in-place hair, an aristocrat's nose, a model's cheekbones, a gentle smile. In some of the pictures she stood next to two teenage boys who looked a lot like her. In many of the portraits she was alone, always smiling, with her mouth anyway; sometimes her eyes had a dazed, haunted look.

"You're looking for something to buy in Santa Fe?" Jorge Mondragon asked watching me quizzically as I sat down across the desk from him. "East Side or West?" I probably didn't look like I had the money for either.

"Actually, I'm not a buyer."

"Then what can I do for you?" he asked, spreading his long fingers and tapping the tips together, anticipating probably that I was going to try to sell him something, advertising or pencils with his name on them.

"I want to talk to you about the Historic Preservation Board."

"Why?" This complicated the matter for him, as I certainly didn't look like I owned a building downtown. He probably already knew all those owners anyway; had approved a few of their plans, turned down a lot more. He picked a pencil up from his desk and began turning it over in his long fingers. LAND OF ENCHANTMENT REAL ESTATE, the white pencil said in black letters, JORGE MONDRAGON, BROKER.

"I'm a friend of Lonnie Darmer's, the woman who . . ."

"I know who Lonnie Darmer was."

"Her family has hired me to investigate her death."

"A private eye?" He smiled a ghost of a smile.

"A lawyer."

"Oh." The smile faded away. Apparently he didn't feel any reciprocal sympathy for my profession. His long fingers laid the pencil down on the desk and were momentarily still. "This has nothing to do with me."

"Well, you approved the First Building, Lonnie campaigned against it, she died." That was as much aggression as I was capable of in this sepulcher of an office.

"You're suggesting she committed suicide because I approved a building?" Jorge Mondragon raised some elegant eyebrows. "In my experience people don't kill themselves over buildings. Love, yes, not buildings."

"I'm not suggesting that she killed herself at all."

"What then?"

What indeed? A shaft of afternoon sun snuck through the grillwork, entered the office and backlit his silvery hair. It made him look too ethereal for a murderer or a real estate broker. "I'm not suggesting anything," I said. "I don't know for sure how or why she died. The family wants to know why the building was approved when there has been so much opposition to the project. I've seen the model myself and I have to say it's very large for Santa Fe; ugly besides."

"If it's the size you're worried about, you've come to the wrong place. Size is regulated by the zoning commission and that building conforms. The ordinance specifies that you can build to a height of sixty-five feet, the height the ladders of the fire trucks would reach at the time the ordinance was put into effect. It is also the height of La Fonda. Are you familiar with that building?"

"Of course."

"Do you think it's ugly?"

"No."

"Looks like it has been there forever, doesn't it?"

"Yes."

"People will say the same thing about the First Building someday. They will also say that it adds to the tax base and provides badly needed jobs and office space. If you ask me the protestors are trying to stop progress. Besides, the zoning commission doesn't have the right to reject projects that comply with the ordinance. That would be an abuse of their power and illegal as well. Of course you're a lawyer; you already know that, don't you?" The light crossed the wrought-iron bars of the window and moved on. The ethereal silver halo was no longer blinding me to the lines of defeat and yearning in his face and he began to look less like a saint, more like a real estate broker. Someone who can convince you that the shabby looks good, the affordable is palatable, a fixer-upper makes a great starter home and three points are not too much to pay for a fixed-rate mortgage.

"The HPB does have the power and the responsibility to turn down a project for aesthetic reasons, and that building is going to be ugly," I responded.

"Ugliness is in the eye of the beholder, isn't it?" He glanced toward the pictures of the woman, who would not be ugly by any standards. "The building complies with the aesthetic standards set by other downtown buildings, it has the puddled adobe look."

"It has the penitentiary look if you ask me. The proportions are terrible, the building is too massive, the windows too small, the courtyard too large."

"With all due respect, I don't think you would like it if

an architect tried to tell you how to practice law." He picked the pencil up again and began tapping the eraser against the desk, softly like everything else he did.

"That's different. Nobody could ever figure out the workings of the law unless they spent years studying it, but anybody can look at a building."

"But everybody sees it differently, don't they? I happen to like the small windows. I find them snug and appealing."

He probably found this damp room with its two-minute daily ration of sun snug and appealing, too. "There was quite a division of opinion among the board, wasn't there?" I asked.

"There was some disagreement."

"And you had the deciding vote?"

"Yes." He put the pencil down, spread his hands, tapped the fingers together and looked toward the corner as if anticipating the moment when he could be all alone with his shrine again. "Is that all?"

"For the moment I guess it is. She's lovely," I pointed to the shrine. "Your wife?"

"Yes. Maria Mercedes. Her nickname was Mecha, which means wick. She was the light of my life but now she's gone. God rest her soul."

"What happened?"

"Cancer." So it was grief that had muted him. "She died a lingering, painful, you could say ugly death. Her hair, her beautiful thick hair came out in handfuls, she weighed eighty pounds, her skin was paper-thin and she was too weak to even lift her hand from the bed. Death is not beautiful. If you will excuse me now I have some business to take care of."

"Thank you for your time."

He waved a weary hand. "It's nothing," he said.

10

It was a relief to get out of the gloom of Mondragon's office and back onto the sunny Paseo, where tourists were smiling for each other's cameras and the shadows were four o'clock long. There was no reason to hurry back to the Duke City—I wasn't going to see the Kid till tomorrow—so I walked a few blocks to the library and looked up Marci Coyle's address in the phone book. She lived on Canyon Road, on the fashionable East Side. It's my theory of urban civilization that the rich and established settle on the east sides of cities and the poor and artistic on the west, but I haven't been all over the world yet to prove it. I decided to walk up to Marci Coyle's and see if she was home; there's never anyplace to park on Canyon Road anyway. I walked past the restaurants, shops and art galleries whose discreet nameplates indicated they weren't interested in my business. Eventually the road becomes residential and two-way, although it's barely wide enough for one. The houses are old here and adobe, the walls come right up to the street and the house numbers are Mexican tile embedded in the walls like they are in Lonnie's neighborhood. It's only a couple of miles in distance but light years away in status and wealth.

Spring had come to Canyon Road. Forsythias were in bloom and junipers were sending out clouds of pollen. A woman in a white dress, white hat and white boots walked down the road pulling a white Scottie behind her. Santa Fe brings out the actress in women. Two old Hispanic men stood across the road talking. They'd probably grown up in this neighborhood before it became chic and their parents and grandparents could well have grown up here, too. A brown mutt belonging to one of the men hung around waiting for them to finish up. When it saw the white dog it lifted its leg and peed.

If there's a leash law in Santa Fe, it's enforced about as often as the speed limit. The woman in white passed by pulling her dog, a black Saab came down Canyon, a camouflage-colored Mercedes-Benz jeep—the car of the moment here and worth about fifty thou—came up. Just before the vehicles squeezed by each other, the mutt saw me and dashed across the road to say hello, coming all too close to getting squashed by the wheel of the jeep. I grabbed him by his collar and yanked him into a narrow space between the road and a wall. "Careful, pooch," I said. "Those Mercedes are killers." The Saab squeezed through and kept on going, but the Merccdes-Benz, whose plates bore the emblem of the Lone Star State, stopped.

Marci Coyle happened to be at the wheel with every hair sprayed in place like she'd just left the hairdresser. She was wearing a signature red warmup suit, although I doubted if she'd been running; the sweats were too neat, the makeup too perfect, and the scarf around her neck seemed a little dressy for the occasion. The well-groomed effect was spoiled, however, by an ugly expression. As she looked at the Hispanic men, then at me, anger distorted her eyes and her mouth swung out of control. "Keep your fucking dog out of the road," she yelled.

"It's not my dog," I answered reasonably.

"If you're not willing to take care of your goddamn fucking dog, then you ought to put it to sleep."

"It's not my dog," I repeated, a little less reasonably, looking to the men for help, but they just watched this exchange as if to say, What could you expect from a Texan? I had to wonder why Marci was taking it out on me. Since we hadn't been introduced at the opening, I had no reason to think she knew who I was. It could be because she was pissed and I was there, but then why not scream at the Hispanic men? They were there, too; the dog had come from them. Maybe she thought they were gentlemen and she didn't want to embarrass herself in front of them, or maybe she thought they were not and was afraid of their reaction. As a female I made a better target. Women always do, even to other women, because we are conditioned not to fight back.

While she glared at me and vented her jets I got a good look at the inside of the camouflage jeep. The seats were glove-soft leather, and there was a bag from the Collected Works bookstore on the floor and another from Origins.

"Goddamn fucking dogs," she said, in case I hadn't heard her the first or second time. She rammed the car into gear, ground a pound out of the transmission and took off. I held the dog until she was safely on her way and then I let him go. He wagged his tail and loped across the road to the men, who patted his head and went on talking.

I continued up Canyon Road and when I saw the jeep parked in a driveway I turned in. Fortunately Marci had left the gate open. She lived in what is known here as a compound, meaning she had more than one building behind her wall, a primary residence and at least one other that was a guesthouse, an artist's studio or just a place to store all the stuff that wouldn't fit in the main house. It had what they call LOSFC, Lots of Old Santa Fe Charm. Daffodils and crocuses were in bloom, a forsythia blazed. The main house was low and sprawling, with soft adobe corners and a line of cow skulls embedded in its front wall. I went up to a hand-carved wooden door, lifted the head of a brassy lion and knocked.

Marci was not pleased—in fact she was downright unpleasant when she found me at her door. "What do *you* want?" she snapped.

"I'm Neil Hamel," I replied, "an old friend of Rick's and Lonnie Darmer's, too, a lawyer in Albuquerque. I want to talk to you."

"About what?"

"Rick." It wasn't entirely true, but it got me through the door. I could see her mentally running through a list of the women Rick had told her about and not finding my name on it. She was insecure enough about him, though, to let me in.

I followed her black Reeboks down a hallway where Sombrajes, shutters made of twigs, cast slender V-shaped shadows on the floor. She led me into a living room that was bigger than Lonnie's half a house and my apartment combined. A baby grand piano was lost in the corner. Oriental rugs were scattered across the quarry-tiled floor. The beams in the ceiling were old and round. There were some large Indian pots that were worth more than my car. A pile of antlers formed an intricate chandelier and a couple more made the backbone of a chair I had no intention of sitting in. A skull with long horns hung over the kiva fireplace. Marci, it seemed, was into bones.

"How do you know Rick?" she asked. She was having trouble deciding which face to put on, hostile or cool.

Scared might have been an option, too, but that wasn't a face she was likely to wear in public.

"We met about fifteen years ago when we lived in San Miguel de Allende," I replied. Marci sat down in one large plush armchair and I in another.

"Mexico," she shrugged as if anything that happened in that place didn't count.

"Lonnie was a friend of mine, too. She and I kept in touch after we moved to New Mexico, but I haven't seen much of Rick."

"Rick has put those days behind him."

"I saw him at the wake."

"I told him not to go, but he seemed to feel it was necessary." She began examining the lacquered finish of a long, red fingernail.

"He's known the Darmers for a long time. He told me how happy he was with the First Building and that you two were getting married."

"Rick said that?" she smiled, more pleased, probably, than she should have been. When she wasn't screaming at strangers, Marci had a confident and successful manner, a polished facade. She was probably superconfident when dealing with bankers, brokers and builders, but loving a guy like Rick was letting termites into the cellar. Sooner or later he'd undermine your foundation. She offered something like an apology for her performance on Canyon Road. "Those damn Hispanics let their dogs run all over the place then slash your tires if you complain."

It explained why she yelled at *me*, but if she thought I was going to join her in condemning Hispanics, she was mistaken. "When I saw Rick he seemed worried about the campaign to stop the First Building and the buttons people have been wearing," I said.

"People can wear all the buttons they want to. The project has been approved; it'll be built."

"It doesn't bother you to be involved in such an unpopular project?"

"Who is it unpopular to? We're providing jobs that this town needs badly. The building is already 90 percent leased to some prestigious clients, the law firm of Lovell, Cruse, Vigil and Roberts, for one. Soon we'll be turning tenants away. That's unpopular? There are people in this town who would be happier communicating through the pony express than a fax machine, but someone is always trying to stop progress; I don't let it stand in my way."

"That's what Jorge Mondragon said."

"Jorge Mondragon? How do you know him?"

"I just went to see him in his office."

"What for?" she asked, attempting to powder herself with bland indifference.

"Lonnie's parents don't believe her death was a suicide or an accident and they hired me to investigate."

"So what does that have to do with Jorge Mondragon or me?"

I took a deep breath and jumped in. "As you know, Lonnie was opposed to your building. She told me Mondragon had been paid off to approve it and that she had proof."

"That drunken bitch," she snapped hard enough to shake the powder off. "What proof could she possibly have of anything? That poor man has had enough problems with his wife dying. You ought to consider the source before you go around accusing people. Lonnie Darmer was a substance abuser and jealous as hell that I am marrying Rick. People like that lose touch with reality. She'd have done anything to discredit me if she thought she could get away with it. You can take it from me, there was no payoff, no proof of anything. That building was approved because it is an excellent project and good for Santa Fe. Didn't Jorge Mondragon tell you that?"

"Yes."

"See?" All that proved to me was that they'd coordinated their stories.

"What do you think happened to Lonnie?" I asked.

"People who live on the edge fall off." She shrugged. The cordless phone on the end table rang and she picked it up. Marci, who wasn't the kind of person to be far from a phone, listened briefly, said, "I'll have to call you back," and hung up.

"You were out of town that weekend, according to Rick," I continued.

"I had business in Dallas."

"When did you get back?"

"Sunday night." The phone rang again. "That's probably my lawyer. I'm expecting an important call from him."

"Lovell, Cruse?" I asked.

"Baxter, Johnson," she replied. "Is there anything else?"

"No, but I'd like to use the bathroom before I leave."

"Down the hallway, second door on the right." She waved her manicured hand in that direction and glanced at her watch as she picked up the phone, probably checking how many minutes her lawyer was charging her for at three to four dollars per. "Garland," she said, not wasting one expensive second, "I need those leases and I need them now."

I made my way down the hallway to the king-size bathroom. There were yellow roses on the vanity, the light was subdued enough to make a person look ten years younger, the Mexican tiles had yellow birds on them, the toilet seat was up.

On my way out, I passed the living room where Marci, oblivious to me, drummed her nails on the coffee table and argued with her lawyer. I let myself out the front door and walked down the path that led to the driveway. The Mercedes jeep wasn't visible from the house. I didn't think the auto alarm would be on at home and Marci's phone conversation had sounded like it would cost her a few hundred dollars more before it was done, so I took a chance and opened the jeep's door. The packages were still on the floor. The book was *The Shell Seekers*, the sales slip was dated today. In the Origins package I found a wearable-art sweater decorated with feathers and tufts of fur that she had—incredibly—paid $700 for, also today. Nobody was screaming at me to stop my investigations yet, so I opened the glove compartment and took a look. There were Texas maps, New Mexico maps, a Mercedes-Benz manual, registration and proof of insurance, some ballpoint pens, a small notebook where Marci kept track of her business mileage, some country-and-western tapes—Reba McEntire and Willie Nelson—and at the very bottom of the pile a parking ticket for an offense that took place on San Francisco Street at 4 P.M. on March 17, the night before Lonnie died.

The sun was setting as I walked back down Canyon. Dogs barked, burglar alarms went off—the songs Santa Fe sings at dusk. High up in the jet stream a plane headed south, leaving a trail of Vs behind it.

11

The Kid and I took Saturday afternoon off and spent it in
bed. That night he played the accordion at El Lobo. He has
a key, and I went to bed early kind of hoping he'd come
back later and let himself in. It was, after all, the second
week of spring. I was asleep and somewhere else, someplace green and fertile, a rain forest, maybe, when he
crawled into bed and woke me with a kiss. He was dressed
and his jacket had the rough texture of an adventure and
an unfamiliar smell of beer and smoke. Suddenly I was
kissing a stranger in my bed; it put a different spin on
things. "Chiquita," he whispered, and I knew it was my
Kid. He got up and I watched him take off his clothes in
the light from the parking lot that filtered through the
drapes and found hollows in his skinny body I'd never
noticed.

"Kid, I want to try something," I said when he was
curled up beside me cool and naked. "Feel these places here
on my neck where my heart beats."

"Yeah, I feel them. You have a strong heart."

"Those are the carotid arteries. They say if you press down on them during sex it makes it really intense. You do it right before you . . ."

"You finish?"

"Yeah."

"You do that too hard you kill somebody."

"I want you to try it later on when I'm . . ."

"You want me to do *that?*"

"Yeah."

"No."

"C'mon, Kid. I know you won't hurt me."

"No."

"Why?"

"What's wrong with us the way it is?"

"Nothing. It's wonderful the way it is, you know that. I'm just curious, that's all. It's something people do; I want to see what it's like."

"What people?"

What was I supposed to say? Killers, rapists, horny teens? That I wanted to see what it felt like to be a murderer's or rapist's victim? That I wanted to see what that victim would do? "Just people."

"Not me. I won't do it."

"Why?"

"It's crazy."

"C'mon."

"No. I'm going to sleep."

That was the end of a promising beginning. The Kid rolled over and pulled the covers around his head. When he does that, there's no talking to him before morning. I waited a few minutes until he went to sleep—it doesn't take long—and then I got up, went into the bathroom and lay down in the cold tub. I leaned back, closed my eyes and pressed my hands against the arteries, feeling the steady thumping of my heart. Apparently this cuts off the supply of blood to the brain—sending it elsewhere I suppose. It intensifies erotic sensations, if it doesn't kill you. It took quite a bit of pressure before I felt any lessening of the blood supply. It wasn't a pleasant sensation to have fingers pushing at my veins; if anybody did it to me I'd fight, not yield, but then yielding doesn't come naturally to me. I tried holding my breath next. They say you can only hold your breath till you pass out, then your body automatically takes over and starts breathing again. I held it long enough to see lights in the darkness, but I couldn't stand the smothering sensation any more than the compressing sensation so I started breathing again. I wondered if the brain experienced oxygen deprivation and/or blood deprivation as light and color and ecstatic vision. It could be the source of mystical experiences, magical orgasms and maybe the being of light after death, as well. But what lay beyond the light and the ecstasy? Darkness and nothing? Those were questions that could only be answered by the very experimental or the very dead.

I got up, went back to bed, curled up behind the Kid and snuggled into the feeling of a warm bed in a cold room. I thought about Lonnie surrendering to fear and light in a cold, dark cave. I wrapped my arms around the Kid, lay my cheek against the soft, silky spot on the back of his neck and dreamed about nothing.

In the morning I whispered, "You awake, Kid?" We forgot about the night before and made careful love. It was Sunday and we couldn't linger; the Kid had cars to work on, although not mine—the part hadn't shown up yet. I invited him for dinner later.

I went to the Albuquerque flea market to see Pete Vigil. There's a flea market outside of Santa Fe, too, right next to the opera and known to some as Der Fledermarket. It's on land the opera patrons probably wish they'd had the fore-sight to buy, a spectacular site with long views of the high mesas. In Santa Fe they sell junk in scenes of breathtaking beauty. Albuquerque's flea market is on the state fair-grounds with a view of resting elephants and a parking lot that's bigger than the Dallas Cowboys'. I parked in the first space I found, which was far, far away, and walked across the lot. A big dusty wind blew around telling me that spring was here, but I already knew that. I entered at the sign that says LIQUOR, GUNS, KNIVES AND OTHER WEAPONS WILL NOT BE ALLOWED ON THE GROUNDS, noting that I was armed with none of them.

This is a big flea market that takes place every weekend. It is loosely arranged by subject: Indian jewelry, Anglo jewelry, Kachinas, tires, tools, food, herbs, pottery, kites, books, household stuff, furniture, rugs, jeans, T-shirts, vel-vet art, bones. I went to the velvet art booth first because I like to visit Elvis every now and then to stay in touch, the young Elvis I mean, not the drugged puffball he became. He was hanging between a snarling tiger and a bleeding Jesus, sneering in tacky splendor, his guitar in hand, the collar of his leather jacket turned up, glitter and glitz on black velvet. It would be a change from a pastel R. C. Gorman woman on the wall. This particular booth also represented Harley-Davidson "The Eagle Has Landed" art: bath towels and velvet paintings. A fierce-looking eagle killed a dragon or posed in front of the American flag. Bikers hung around here wearing black leather gloves with the fingers cut out and sleeveless T-shirts that bared their tattooed arms.

The bikers were one kind of American, but there were a lot of other groups represented at the flea market, giving it an international flavor. The dust blowing around added to the Third World feeling. There were West Africans in native dress selling baskets and beads; Southeast Asians walking in groups with their children and speaking a quick, sharp language; lots of Hispanics, some Mexican, some not; many Native Americans. The X-ray light here made everyone look like what they were only more so, and Anglos got bleached white as bone. I saw a girl who had exaggerated her whiteness and made herself into a work of flea-market art—a look Anna would have envied. She had pale skin and long, frizzy blonde hair pulled high up on top of her head and hanging way down her back. She wore a black tube top and skintight spandex pedal pushers, black high heels, bright red nails and lipstick, the female equivalent of Elvis. It takes a certain brassiness to pull the look off. She had it, but so did he and look what happened to him. There were some aging hippies here, as there always are at New Mexico gatherings, dressed in long skirts, ripped jeans, Guatemalan *huipils*. The fine lines etched on their faces were like the thin lines on maps that lead to out-of-the-way pockets, mountain villages, time warps. I wouldn't want to walk around with twenty years of alternate lifestyle written all over me, but then I wouldn't want to walk around with ten years of lawyer written on me either. I'd like to walk around with nothing written—keeping my feet in all possible worlds—but it's hard to pull it off. The flea market makes me glad to be an American; in a way this place is about as American as you can get. I mean border or coastal America anyway, where the Third World pushes at the door.

Making my way to bones, I followed a path through miscellaneous junk and jewelry, and passed a booth of animal skins, furs, bird feathers and belly-up turtle shells. These empty, gawking shells could make you cry for the turtles who'd been forced to vacate them. Next I came to a booth selling chile *ristras*, long strips of dried red chile peppers, some of them arranged into hearts, a Valentine's Day gift for a picante-loving lover. The following booth had red roses for sale, and not the live ones that turn brown and die in two days either. These were pickled roses in a jar, roses that would last forever like the rose the Kid gave me. Maybe he bought it here some weekend and saved it for a special occasion. I'm not the kind of woman to call up a jewelry store and find out how much a lover paid for a ring, or to pick up a rose and look for a price on the bottom of the jar either. A pickled rose on the mantel might be the equivalent of Elvis Presley on the wall but I wouldn't take it down.

In the jewelry section a woman was trying on a silver ring. "It's Navajo," the seller—who wasn't—said. The buyer had decided against it, but was having trouble getting the ring off her finger. "If it doesn't come off, we take the finger," said the Anglo vendor. "If the finger doesn't come off, we take the hand. If the hand doesn't come off, we take the arm. If the arm . . ."

I walked past the clocks with pictures of bleeding Jesuses painted on them, past a guy playing a guitar and foot-powered drum singing early Bob Dylan and a booth selling baby avocados—twelve for a dollar. "Hey, Ma," a Hispanic girl yelled at her mother. "Those avocados are big as your eyeballs." When I got to bones I found Pete Vigil sitting on an aluminum chair behind a blanket with several sets of elk antlers spread across it, wide, white antlers with prongs that reached for the sky. King was not with him.

"Good morning, my friend," Pete said.

"Hello," I replied. "How you doing?"

"Good. And you?"

"Okay. Where's King today?"

"I can't bring him here. He's too macho, he fights with all the other dogs. You want to buy an elk horn? For you it will only be forty dollars."

"They're kind of large. How would I get it home?"

"They fold up. I'll show you." He showed me a joint in

the middle where the horns could be folded together.

"What would I do with it?"

"Put it over your fireplace. This is a good one here. It has twelve prongs. Every year they lose the horns and in the spring the velvet comes back. I can give you this one for thirty-five dollars."

"I'll think about it," I said. "I have a lot of things on my mantel already."

"A picture of your boyfriend?"

"Yup."

"When we get married you'll have to take him down."

"I'm getting kind of used to him."

"I'm sorry to hear that." Pete Vigil sighed. "I wanted you all to myself. The man you want to see is at the end of the aisle here on the left. Just tell him I sent you."

"I will. Thanks a lot."

"Come back and tell me what he says."

"Okay," I answered. Pete Vigil was a charming man, but an old man who'd mastered the skills lonely old people have for grabbing your attention and holding it. I hoped the bone man wouldn't be a wasted effort, a fiction Pete had created to bring some adventure to his life.

The bone man's specialty was antlers and skulls. He had a lot of them and they were spread over a large blanket, white skulls with gaping black holes in the middle of the forehead and where the eyes had been. Some had been painted with blue or red designs. Some had horns attached, some seemed to be horses or cattle, the kind of cattle you come across in the national forest that are put out to graze in the spring and get rounded up in the fall but don't always make it back.

He was a medium-size Anglo about my age. His dark hair was pulled into two ponytails and wrapped in leather thongs. He wore a T-shirt and leaned against a rotting brown pickup that would be a sure bet in the Taos ugly truck contest. Some feathers tied onto the door handle and the antenna flapped in the breeze. He faced west like a dog with his nose to the wind so all I could see was profile. I waited for him to turn around, looked at the bones, sent a telepathic message that I was there. When that didn't work, I said, "Excuse me."

He pulled himself away from the truck and ambled over. As he turned toward me I could see that his T-shirt had a map of a once-familiar stain of a country on it. SOUTHEAST ASIA WAR GAMES, the shirt said, 1959–1975. SECOND PLACE. "You into bones?" he asked me.

"At the moment," I said. "Where do you get all these skulls from anyway?"

"I find them, people sell them to me. Why do you want to know?"

Why indeed? Was I expecting him to say he killed animals just to get their bones? "Just curious, I guess. Who buys them?"

"Anybody and everybody."

"What do they do with them?"

"Hang 'em on the walls, make chandeliers, makes no difference to me. And you? You lookin' or buyin'?" He pulled a toothpick out of his jeans pocket.

"Neither. Pete Vigil sent me."

"Oh, yeah." He put the toothpick between his teeth and began to chew. "His son was my buddy in Nam."

"So he said."

"I'm workin' on it, I hang out, hear things. Give me your number, and I'll call if I get something definite."

I handed him one of my lawyer's cards and he took it with his left hand and stuck it in the pocket of his jeans. "This case is very important to me," I said. "I need all the help I can get. I'm representing the victim's family and I'm not getting any cooperation from the police."

125

"There when you don't want 'em, not there when you do," he said.

"The sooner you could call me, the better."

"Hey, I said I'll do what I can." As he bent over to rearrange a skull, I saw a dark spot around his elbow that resembled a bruise but turned out to be a spiderweb tattoo with an insect trapped in it.

"That's an interesting tattoo. A spiderweb, right?"

"Right."

"What's the insect?"

"A fly that got caught in the web."

"Where'd you get it?"

"The fly?"

"The tattoo."

"Why? You want one?" He looked me over from top to bottom, side to side, looking for the right spot, maybe, to place a tattoo.

"Just curious."

"I got mine in Da Nang, but you can get 'em here now."

"Well, thanks for your help."

"Yeah." He walked away, leaned against the pickup and turned his nose back to the wind. I returned to Pete Vigil, who was sitting in his aluminum chair resting his head in his hands like he'd fallen asleep.

"Wake up, Pete," I said.

He started, but smiled when he saw me. "How did you make out?"

"Well, he didn't reveal anything, but said he'd call me."

"He won't tell you much, but he won't tell you wrong either. You didn't buy any bones from him, did you?"

"Nope."

"Good. I've been thinking about it. I can let you have this antler here for thirty dollars. That's a real bargain for twelve prongs."

"I'll think it over," I said. "Thanks, Pete."

"It's a pleasure," he replied.

I went out through the jewelry section. The woman who had been trying to get the silver ring off had succeeded and the Anglo jeweler was trying to sell it to someone else. "That one's Hopi," he said. Navajo one minute, Hopi the next. I went back to the parking lot and tried to find my car, which was like looking for one of those cows in the fall that had been let loose in the national forest in spring. I'd forgotten that I wasn't driving a beat-up old and ugly orange Rabbit any longer, but a new white Ford just like everybody else. I didn't remember what row it was in, only that it was at the far end of the lot. There were a lot of white Fords at that end of the lot and a number of them had false plates on the front that said RICH FORD if they didn't say EL JEFE or DOREEN. "God damn it," I told myself. "You've got better things to do than look for a stupid car," but that's what I was doing, walking up one aisle and down the next, looking for a white Ford that my key would fit in because I didn't have any other way to identify it. It made a good case for tying a feather to the antenna or hanging a pair of signature fuzzy dice from the mirror. A jet flew overhead and left a squiggly trail in the sky, a low rider cruised by with something chrome and glittery spinning inside the wheel rims, a pickup passed me with a license plate that had a purple heart on it and a bumper sticker that said VIETNAM . . . The rest was in Navajo.

Eventually I found a lock that fit my key and promised myself that from now on I would make a note of where I left the legger. I went home and took a nap, and when I woke up made chile willies for the Kid. It's a mixture of salsa, blue corn tortillas and cheese, his favorite meal of the ones I make. He brought the Tecate and the limes.

"Kid," I asked him over dinner at my coffee table. "Are you going to be getting the part for *el conejo* soon? A white car in a parking lot is like a deer in the woods. You can't find it."

"The guy promised me just a few more days, Chiquita. The white car's not so bad."

"You'd look good in it, Kid. I don't."

"How do you look?"

"Like a lawyer on white bread."

"You are a lawyer."

"Maybe, but who wants to look like one?" There was a red rose on the mantel, picante food and the Kid at the coffee table, me in the middle.

The Kid shrugged. "You can't drive an old car forever, Chiquita. Maybe it's time to get a new one."

"I can't afford it."

"*El conejo* will cost you a lot of money, if you keep it. When they get old it's one thing after another."

"I know. Listen, Kid, I want to ask you something. Do you think I'm bland? I went to the flea market today and everybody there looked a lot more interesting than me."

"Bland? What does that mean?"

"It means a boring white person with no tribe, no history, no family, no color."

"You, Chiquita? Bland? *Tienes pelotas.*" That means "you have balls," it's one of those idioms that translate literally from one language to another. "You are independent, brave."

The trouble with being brave and independent is that you can't be colorful, too. It's fun to dress up in tribal costume when you're with your tribe, but it's crazy to attract attention when you're out there on the firing line alone.

"To me you are . . . you are very . . ." The Kid picked up his Tecate, sipped, thought.

What? I wondered. Bitter, smart-ass?

"American," he said.

12

On Monday morning I called Bunny Darmer in Roswell. She'd been patient, but it had been four days since I'd agreed to represent her and I knew she'd want to hear what had been accomplished. I was relieved technology hadn't gotten to the point yet where you have to look at who you're talking to. I wasn't eager to enter Bunny's kitchen or bedroom and see her slumped over the phone in her old bathrobe with her hair matted gold and gray.

"I was hoping you'd call today," she said in a flat, quiet voice. "If you didn't I was going to call you."

"How are you doing?"

"It's not getting any better."

"I'm sorry." I couldn't really know what Bunny felt, but what could be worse than losing a child? It had to be a whole other dimension of pain, the outer edge of the pain envelope. I imagined it might be something like living in the far north in the fall when the days get shorter and the nights longer and you're moving toward the solstice, the point where you're submerged in night. If you live through it, spring will come. But until you've been there, you can't imagine how dark it will be and once you're in the depths, it's hard to believe it will ever get brighter. The only way to find out what you can endure is to endure it. That's what Bunny had to look forward to.

"She has clothes here in her closet," she said. "I go in there and I look at them and I think, she will never wear that shirt, she will never wear that sweater, she'll never wear any of them ever again."

"I have a sweater of hers that I borrowed. Would you like it back?" Bunny hadn't mentioned her daughter's name and I found that I couldn't say it either, as if naming her violated some primitive and sacred taboo.

"No, you keep it. Who have you talked to so far?" she asked.

"Rick; his fiancée and backer Marci Coyle; and Jorge Mondragon, who approved the building." It wasn't really a lawyer's role to be conducting an investigation, but that's what I'd been doing. "Nobody's admitting to anything."

"What about the police, did you talk to them?"

"Yes, but first I saw a friend of mine who used to be a medical investigator. He told me it's possible she could have been murdered with no signs."

"How?"

"Smothered," I said and left it at that.

"And did you tell Railback?"

"Yes, and I took him the knob from the sleeping bag that I found, too. He still doesn't think there was any crime."

"That . . . that . . ." I could have filled in the blanks for her easily. Shit. Prick. Son of a bitch. "Rat," she said. If I hadn't given her hope, I'd given her anger—at least it would get her through the day. If it would make her feel better to blame him, like Railback himself had said, so be it. "*He* can just close his file and say it's over. But it will

130

never be over for us. Never. She was our only child. When you only have one your whole life revolves around her and what she will do."

"Believe me, she'd have done a lot by stopping the building. I've seen the model and it is ugly. But people are still campaigning against it, and I hope they'll succeed. Fortunately Railback's not our last alternative. I talked to Dennis Quinlan, the district attorney, and he's going to look into it."

"Good. It sounds like you've been busy."

I had been when you stopped to think about it. "I want to talk to Lonnie's friend Ci next."

"Keep me informed, please."

"I will," I said.

Monday afternoon found me on the lonesome highway for another visit to Rick. Good Friday was only four days away and the *peregrinos* were starting out, with a couple of miles behind them and eighty or ninety to go, men usually, alone or in pairs, ordinary, dumpy and out-of-shape guys carrying day packs and water jugs, walking briskly along the shoulder of the interstate while the cars and the semis whizzed by. They were headed for the sanctuary at Chimayo to dip into the chapel's healing earth, give thanks and/or ask for forgiveness. Religion is taken seriously in northern New Mexico; the more difficult the journey, the greater the reward. Except for the highway overpasses there's not a patch of shade on the interstate, and at five thousand to seventy-five hundred feet the sun doesn't let you forget it. Some *peregrinos* wore hats, some wrapped their heads in scarves desert style, some were bareheaded. It was a little after one, the sun was close to midheaven, their shadows were lumps of darkness at their heels. A lot of the *peregrinos* were probably atoning for a year of wife and/or substance abuse, but you had to admire the effort.

I got to Santa Fe a little early for my appointment with Rick, so I stopped at the De Vargas Mall to get a midafternoon sugar fix. At Albertson's I had to wait on a long line to pay for a solitary bag of M&Ms. I usually don't go grocery shopping in the afternoon, and I'd forgotten that it takes all afternoon to do it. People who are free in the daytime are a different breed than the working class. There are a lot of them in Santa Fe, writers, maybe, artists, as well as the ungainfully unemployed. Albertson's, on the cutting edge of supermarket technology, had installed a new checkout system, a robot under the counter who announced what you had bought and how much it cost in flight-attendant voice. "Bananas, forty cents a pound," it droned, "coffee, four ninety-eight, OBs, five ten, Preparation H, five-fifty." It was enough to send you back to work.

So were the guys hanging around the parking lot. I'd made a note of where I'd left the car this time and went right to it, keys in hand, which is a good place for them. A couple of men were leaning on a nearby ugly truck. I was aware of their presence, but I don't look too closely at idle men in parking lots. I know what they're going to look like anyway. Those are the kind of guys who consider a casual look an invitation and eye contact a signed deal. The kind who will insult you, rape you (mentally if not physically) and never hike to Chimayo to apologize.

"You got big tits," said one of them as I stuck the key in the lock.

"You've got a big mouth," I foolishly replied.

"I got a big pecker, too."

"Why don't you put it where your mouth is?"

"I'd like to put it in your . . ."

I got in, slammed the door, turned the radio loud, put my foot to the floor and burned rubber getting out of there.

It didn't put me in the best mood for meeting Rick in his territorial office. He was sitting behind his desk with his gray hair in place, his expression under control. His hair had once been long, black and curly, but even then he wore it tied back in a ponytail. His eyes had always been speckled blue and evasive. "My old friend Neil," he smiled tightly, indicating he was still pissed at me for insulting his building, but if I'd told him then and there (falsely) that I was sorry, that I regretted deeply having insulted him, that, even after all these years, I remembered him as a wonderful, magical lover, he would have forgiven me. Not only that, he probably would have suggested we go off somewhere and do it again. That's the kind of guy he was, as enslaved to the chase and to women—or his concept of himself in relationship to women—as individual women were to him. "What do you want?" he asked in a voice that was just expressionless enough to allow any possibility.

"How well do you know Jorge Mondragon?" I asked.

"For Christ's sake, Neil, forget about it. Lonnie self-destructed, nobody murdered her, nobody paid Jorge Mondragon off. Not me, not Marci, not anybody. She told me you'd been at the house asking questions. What's this obsession with playing amateur dick? You bored with being a lawyer? You need the Darmers' money or just feeling guilty because *you* were the one who let Lonnie go off alone and stoned?"

I kept my cool. "I believe my question was 'How well do you know Jorge Mondragon?'"

"I know about him—this isn't that big a town—but I don't know him personally. The only time I ever actually met him was at the hearing. Okay?"

"How long has he been a real estate broker?"

"Couple of years, I guess."

"What did he do before that?"

"Worked for the state."

"So he's not exactly loaded."

"No, but he's not starving either. He's lived here all his

life, he probably bought a house for thirty thou thirty years ago that's worth ten times that now."

"His wife's illness must have been costly."

"That's what people have insurance for."

"People who work for themselves don't always have insurance. Maybe he was starting a new business, putting everything into it, and he couldn't afford the premiums at first. Maybe he started a new policy and his wife's illness fell under the preexisting condition clause." Our health insurance system has a crack running right through the middle of it. I knew that because I was one of those who'd fallen through. "You're self-employed, how many years have you gone without insurance?" I asked him.

"A lot," he admitted. "I couldn't afford it."

"See?"

"I didn't pay Jorge Mondragon off. Okay? My building is good, it stands on its own merits, I didn't have to pay anyone off. As a matter of fact, even if I'd wanted to, I don't have the money to pay anyone off. I don't even have the money to pay *you* to go away and leave me alone." He stood up and began pacing the floor in his black Reeboks.

"I wouldn't say Marci was poverty-stricken."

"Marci didn't pay him off either. Believe me, I'd know it if she did."

"Maybe you don't know everything there is to know about Marci Coyle." I felt through my bag searching for the parking ticket.

"What have you been doing? Following her? Taking pictures? Pursuing your private-eye fantasy? Too bad you never went to the trouble to find work that was satisfying, Neil. That's the point of having a career, isn't it? Not just to work, but to love the work you're doing?"

I could have said that's the point of making love, isn't it? Not just to do it, but to love—or at least like and respect—the person you're doing it with? But I stuck to my business.

"The Mercedes-Benz is Marci's car, right?"

"Yeah."

"Do you ever drive it?"

"No. I have a BMW." She *gave* him a BMW would probably be more like it. I took the ticket out of my purse and laid it on his desk. "What's this?" he asked.

"A parking ticket for the Mercedes."

He looked at the ticket and saw I was right. "Big deal. She was parked in front of some stud's place? Is that it?"

"No, she was parked on West San Francisco."

"So?"

"It isn't the place that makes it interesting, it's the date. See? March seventeenth."

"So what?"

"Lonnie died that night."

"And?"

"You told me Marci went to Texas that weekend."

"I did. Oh, shit." He buried his head in his hands and when he looked up again the robin's eggs had cracks in them. "I . . . um . . . I lied, Neil."

What else was new? He'd always lied. "You mean she *didn't* go to Texas that weekend?"

"No, not about that. I thought she went. I . . . um . . . I lied to Marci. I wasn't home that night. I went out."

"Where?"

"It was nothing, someone I met at Club West."

"Someone? Just someone?"

"Yeah. No threat to Marci. Honest. God, I hope she didn't stay here to check up on me. Do me a favor, for old times' sake, please don't tell her I told you this. Even if she asks."

"Do *me* a favor, will you? Put that ticket back in her glove compartment before she notices it's missing, at the bottom under all the other stuff." It was evidence. I could have turned it over to Detective Railback, but he was unlikely to be impressed and I had come by it illegally. It was also evidence he could obtain easily enough himself . . . if he chose to. Besides, I'd made myself a copy.

"What? Oh, yeah, okay." He'd put his head back in his hands again. It was a good performance, but the trouble with liars is that they can be lying even when they are confessing to lying. Philanderers lie, criminals lie—it went with the territory. Even if you know liars are lying, you don't necessarily know what they're covering up. Was he protecting her? Him? Both of them? Was Lonnie the someone he'd met at Club West? It was a quagmire and I wanted out of there, because no matter what Rick told me about March 17, I'd never believe him. Besides, I'd said what I had to say.

There was a clock on his desk, a black plastic model that flashed red numbers. Three o'clock. The afternoon was shot anyway, there was no point in rushing back to my office, and there was one person I hadn't spoken to yet. "Do you happen to know where Ci lives?" I asked.

"At the end of Pajaro off Old Santa Fe Trail, the last house on the right."

I passed the model on my way out—I had to, it filled most of the reception room. It had gotten bigger, lumpier, uglier.

Along with the shops that sell howling coyotes, slithering snakes and turquoise jewelry, the Mile High running-shoe store was a few blocks from Rick's office. I walked over there, went in and picked up a pair of black Reeboks, the shoes Rick and Marci, the power couple, wore. They were selling for the incredible—to me anyway—price of $64.99. I looked at the rubber sole. It had a series of wavy lines indicating moving water or air, not the Vs of birds in flight.

"Can I help you?" asked the clerk, the kind of semi-fit, semi-athletic, semi-inconspicuous guy who lurks in running-shoe stores.

136

"Maybe," I replied. "I like a certain type of cleat in my running shoe, one that's shaped like a V. It's kind of a quirk of mine. Does Reebok make any like that?"

"You mean like a V on the bottom of the shoe?"

"Yeah, that's what I mean."

He shook his head as if to imply that I was one wild and kinky lady. What did he think I did with these shoes anyway? "I don't think so, but why don't we take a look?" He went all around the store picking up Reeboks and Nikes looking loudly for Vs. He picked up an Air Jordan, a Windrunner, a Pegasus. "No, not this one, this one's a square, or maybe it's octagonal. You want to take a look?"

"Octagonal," I said.

Next he picked up a Reebok Pump for $170.

"One hundred and seventy dollars?" I said. "Why would anybody pay that much for a pair of shoes?"

"They've got air," he said.

"Air's free, isn't it?"

"Not in a shoe it isn't."

He looked at every shoe in the store with and without air, but none of them had Vs.

"Well, thanks anyhow," I told him.

"Hey, no trouble. You find a pair, you let me know, okay? I'd like to see those shoes in action."

"Don't let it break your heart," I replied, "but you won't be the first one on my list."

13

Pajaro, the road Ci lived on, was steep, unpaved and patterned with the kind of ruts that said rich people live here.
It's a reverse snobbery they cultivate in Santa Fe—the
more expensive the houses, the bigger the four wheel
drives, the worse the roads. There was a medium-size
Subaru in the driveway and a large gray junker, a low-
slung American model that must have scraped its belly on
the ruts. The site had a spectacular view and the house took
full advantage of it. Not one of those closed-in East Side
adobes, it was new, sprawling, filled with windows and the
latest in solar tech. There were collectors on the roof, a
Trombe wall to grab and hold the sun, a large solarium
filled with plants, ordinary houseplants that had grown to
rain-forest proportions in the controlled environment.
There was a patio on the west side of the house to catch the
sunset and one on the east for the rise. There was probably
a skylight somewhere, too, for looking at *el cielo*.

The doorbell chimed and tinkled. A captive audience, I

had to listen to the performance until Ci answered. "Neil, is it?" she asked when she opened the door. "The woman warrior?"

"You got a few minutes? I'd like to talk to you."

"Of course." She smiled, as if she might even have been expecting me. "Come on in." She led me into an oval living room that opened onto the solarium. There wasn't a square corner in this room; it was all curving lines and there were more windows than walls. The floor was covered with a deep white carpet. The furniture was curved to match the walls, large, white commas of sofas with lavender silk pillows. There wasn't a print or a painting on the white walls, only a lone Indian pot in front of the fireplace. The effect was soothing and expensive and indicated to me that Ci was charging her clients a lot more than the $100 per hour some lawyers in Albuquerque got. Her dressed-for-success look was a broomstick-pleated Navajo skirt made out of metallic silver, material that you'd never find on a reservation. She had a shirt to match and a concho belt over it. Her silver-streaked hair was loose and full, her eyes were turquoise blue. Her bare feet waded through the carpet without a sound. I was aware that my shoes had been sullied by city streets, but I didn't feel like taking them off. I followed her across the room and sat down on a sofa between two lavender pillows.

"Could I have a glass of water?" I asked, having worked up a thirst in the dusty road.

"I didn't have a chance to get to the store today. Sorry. I don't have any."

"You don't have any water?" We were deep in the twentieth century; it had been some time since indoor plumbing had become the basis of Western civilization. As this place was probably worth a cool million, I would have insisted on hot and cold running water, if it had been mine. "What do you use to bathe in, do the dishes, flush the toilet, wash your hair?" I asked.

"I have tap water for those things, but I wouldn't wash my *hair* in it . . ."

"Oh, that's right. You use Perrier, don't you?"

"Evian," she said. "And I don't drink tap water."

I'd lived in Mexico and had every *parásito* known to man, the Santa Fe reservoir didn't scare me. "I'll take a chance," I said.

While she was in the kitchen getting the water a cat strolled into the living room, one of those calm, self-possessed cats that push at the limits of the pet envelope. He had a long, white coat with a lustrous sheen to it—maybe he got washed in Evian, too. This pet was well fed and well cared for and he knew it. I bet there was no smelly Puss 'n Boots getting moldy in his dish. He zeroed in on me, which I expected—cats always go for those of us who are allergic or antagonistic; what I didn't expect was that I'd let him do it. He walked over, jumped into my lap and before I could bounce him out began to purr and rub my hand with his back. It was irresistibly silky and crackled with electricity.

Ci came back with my water. "Get down, Como," she said.

"I don't mind. He has a beautiful coat."

"That's because he doesn't eat meat," she replied.

"How do you keep him away from birds and snakes and mice out here?"

"He doesn't go outside either," she said. "I suppose you came to talk about Lonnie." She curled up on a sofa and tucked her bare feet underneath her, spreading her skirt over them in a sunburst pattern.

I would have liked to cross my legs, but I couldn't with Como on my lap, so like a lady I placed one ankle over the other. "Yes. I was wondering if you saw her or have any idea where she went after the Malones' party."

"She went to the ruins."

"I mean before that."

"My impression was that she left with you."

"She took me to her house, but then she went out on her own. Were you home? Maybe she came here."

"We were home all alone, weren't we, Como?" He purred as if on cue. "Lonnie didn't visit us. Are you conducting an investigation and, if so, may I ask why?"

"The Darmers hired me to look into it."

"Into what? The police said she died peacefully, didn't they? No trauma, no wounds?"

"That's what they said."

"Then those are the facts of her death. Saturn was conjunct her sun in the eighth house, which indicates a death experience. That's a power spot that she died in."

"You've been there?"

"Yes. Both Lonnie and I experienced some powerful past life vibrations in that cave. The way I see it, she had completed this incarnation and done what she came here to do. It was her time to move on."

Assuming that we were here to do anything besides reproduce and consume sugar, that seemed like a large statement to me. "How can you say she'd done what she came here to do?" I asked. "She hadn't stopped the Ugly Building, had she? If there was anything she wanted to do, that was it."

"She set the wheels in motion. It's up to us to finish the work."

"It's pretty hard for the Darmers to accept her death. She was their only child."

"Accept it they must. We will all miss Lonnie; she had a wonderful kind of loving, accepting, but at the same time challenging energy. But it will be very distressing to her spirit if we hold her to the earth plane. Trust me. You will be doing a great harm if you continue this investigation.

Clinging keeps her from moving into the light."

"Into the light?"

"People who have the death experience are met on the other side by the being of light." She smiled as if she'd already been there.

"The Darmers believe Lonnie was murdered," I said.

"How could she have been murdered? Wasn't the cause of death poisons that she voluntarily ingested into her system? And even if she were murdered, her soul chose the moment of her death; it was her destiny. If that happened, the murderer was only the instrument of her destiny."

"She could have been smothered with a pillow," I said, picking up a lavender silk model. "There would have been no marks if she didn't struggle."

"If she didn't struggle, then she acquiesced in her death, didn't she?"

The New Age was beginning to seem pretty heartless to me. "She was drinking and taking Valium and she didn't know what was happening. That doesn't mean she acquiesced."

"The cell's recesses always know what's happening."

Como heard something that struck a chord of fear in his cat consciousness. His ears picked up, and he pressed his claws deep into my thighs to gain a footing, leaped off my lap and dashed across the carpet and out of the room. I flexed my legs to make sure they still worked. He hadn't drawn blood, anyway.

"Oh, Como, Como, Como," Ci said, "you're such a scaredy, scaredy cat."

"What's he scared of?"

"The shadows. Isn't that what everybody's afraid of—the dark? But in the darkness is the light and in the end is the beginning. There is nothing to fear."

It seemed kind of metaphysical for the cat whose long tail was rapidly disappearing around the corner. "Rick First told me that you use pillows to deprive people of oxygen and give them a vision of the next life," I continued. "What do the cell's recesses think while that's happening?"

"Oh, is that stupid rumor circulating again?" She smiled and rearranged the pleats around her legs. "That was started by malicious people years ago, coagulated lumps of spirit, who won't take the trouble to understand my work. Rick First should look into his own heart and see what responsibility he finds there. I don't need cheap parlor tricks to see people's next lives. I can read it in their auras, their gestures, their body language. You, for instance."

"Me?"

"Neil Hamel, Albuquerque attorney. I can see your next life very clearly."

I took a look down that lonesome highway. "Well, I hope I get a car that runs."

"What I see is a more fully developed Venus, the feminine side, the Martian masculine has taken the ascendancy in this lifetime. Your nurturing, mothering, intuitive function is inferior, creating an imbalance, and nature always seeks balance. You will be a mother the next time—not a lawyer. You've gone as far as you can go in that direction."

"There *are* women who are both."

She waved her hand as if to dismiss that lump of thought. "Of course. But you're not one." The doorbell rang, the chimes tinkled around the house. Ci got up and padded over the thick carpet in her bare feet, then across the quarry-tiled entryway. Lonnie's neighbor, Dolby, was at the door, and she let him in. He was wearing a pair of jeans, a long-sleeved flannel shirt, gardener's gloves. He had the smile of an eager, hyperactive stray in search of a meal, a room, a mother.

"Dolby, are you finished already?" Ci asked.

"Sure. Hey," he said, noticing me sitting in the living room. "I know you."

"That's right. We met in the driveway at Lonnie's wake."

"Oh, yeah. That's right, Lonnie's driveway."

Dolby started to enter the room and got as far as the white carpet when Ci stopped him. "Dolby," she scolded, "your shoes."

He looked down at his running shoes whose brand name had been obliterated by red New Mexico mud, but probably wasn't anything to brag about anyway. "What's wrong with my shoes?"

"They're dirty."

Dolby looked at my shoes. "She's wearing shoes, isn't she?"

"Yes," said Ci, "she is."

"*They're* dirty."

"Have you had a reading yet?" I asked to change the subject. Dolby stayed in the entryway with his shoes on, fidgeting. Standing still didn't seem to come easily to him. Too much stored-up teenage testosterone, I guessed.

"Sure. Why not?"

What foundation was he laying with the building blocks of his life? I wondered. "So what's it going to be for you the next time around?"

"A vet or maybe work in a zoo. Ci says I've got some karma to work out with animals."

"Dolby does the yard work around here," she said. "Excuse us for a minute. I want to take a look at what he's done."

"See ya," Dolby said.

" 'Bye," I replied.

Ci put on some Birkenstock sandals she kept by the front door and they went out. I waited, watching a purple Wandering Jew in the sunroom wander an inch further, wishing the cat would come back. "Psst, Como," I whispered, but there was no response. Wherever he'd gone, he was staying put. I heard the sound of voices but not words. A door slammed, a car left. I picked up a lavender pillow, put it down. Ci came back alone, took her sandals off, walked barefoot across the rug.

"How'd he do?" I asked.

"Good," Ci said. "Dolby is a Virgo and can do very meticulous work. He hates to get his hands dirty. This is a pivotal incarnation for him with a lot of karma to work out. He's moved a lot and has had difficulty establishing relationships with people his own age. Somewhere along the way he picked up a conventionally religious mind-set that I am trying to break him out of." It sounded like therapy to me, but I suppose forward life progressions are a therapy of sorts. Even getting someone to listen to you is therapy these days. "Not to change the subject, but would you like to visit the skyviewer while you're here?"

"What's a skyviewer?"

"A sculpture made by an artist I know. I have one out back." Along with the hot tub and the Jacuzzi, probably. "It's a way of looking at a consistent source of light—the sky—until it changes your perceptions."

"You can just walk outside and look at the sky, can't you?" I asked. We were in New Mexico, after all, where the sky speaks loud and clear and often.

"It has a different effect when it's framed. The skyviewer brings the sky down to you. I consider it a sculpture, but the zoning board considered it a building and you wouldn't believe what I had to go through to get a permit. They even dictated what kind of lights we could use inside. Architectural fascism, if you ask me."

Architectural fascism, architectural anarchy, it was hard to tell what you were going to get in this city. They'd nail you for lights in a skyviewer or lavender trim and let an extravagantly large and ugly building go by. "You just sit in this thing and look at the sky?" I asked.

"Yes, but the lighting and the framing change the way you see it. In the daytime you can't see the stars because the sun is out and the sky is too bright, but when it gets dark you can, unless you are in a lit space looking out, then all you see is black. You see incredible colors in the skyviewer, colors that don't exist in art or in nature, colors that exist only in the eye and the mind. Lonnie was into color, you know."

"I know."

"She loved the skyviewer. I think it's something she'd want you to experience. Will you do it?"

"All right," I said.

The skyviewer was built into and on top of a pyramid-shaped mound out back. The entry was cut into the side of the pyramid, and it was framed by a stucco wall. A rectangular box a couple of feet high stood on top of the pyramid. To me it looked like a combination of a Pueblo Indian kiva and a small Mayan temple. The dirt all around it was patterned with the hieroglyphics of running shoes, but none that I recognized. "What do I do?" I asked.

"Just go inside," said Ci. "Sit down, stand up, whatever you feel like doing."

"How long does it last?"

"As long as you want it to," she said. "I usually stay until dark. I'll be inside. Come and share your experience with me before you go."

I walked down a crunchy gravel path, through the side of the pyramid, and I had the sense of entering a ruin, although the building was new. It had been a while since I'd plunked myself down in a ruin and waited to see what happened; I wondered if I was still up to it. The inside of the skyviewer was rectangular, maybe fifteen feet high, with a low bench all around to sit on. A few feet above head level there was a circle of artificial light. Several feet above that was the rectangular ceiling, about twelve feet by ten.

A parallel rectangle had been cut out a few feet into the ceiling and it was open to the sky. It was hard to tell what the ceiling was made out of—metal, maybe. It had a sharp edge. The artist who designed it obviously understood the power of proportion. The skyviewer had the pleasing symmetry of an indigenous structure.

Through the entry passage I could see the sky and through the cut-out ceiling I could also see the sky, but they weren't the same. The entryway's was pale and washed out, an Eastern sky. The ceiling sky was true Western blue. It had to be the lights and framing that made the difference. The interior of the skyviewer was whitewashed like a Greek or Mediterranean building, but at that point it had a diffuse kind of mauvish glow.

The sky slowly deepened and the walls did, too, until they became the color of adobe. The elbow of the adobe-colored ceiling against the sky was Georgia O'Keeffe in color and shape. The sky got bluer, and I had the sensation that I was peering into a box and could see the angle inside where the corners met. I looked away and when I looked up again the sky had entered the room like Ci had said it would. It overlapped the edges of the ceiling and was an overwhelmingly beautiful high-altitude blue. The color was deepest at the corners. You couldn't see anything in it but color—no clouds, no planes, just blue. I wondered if you peeled away a corner of the blue ceiling, what you would find beyond it, pure business, pure white?

I was experiencing the significance of visual distortion, a clear-headed hallucination, so clear that I could be in it and watch myself in it at the same time. The sky got deeper until it became the richest, most incredible blue, the color of ecstasy, the color of choice. I could have spent a lifetime in it, easily. You'd think a New Mexican would know all there was to know about blue, but I'd never seen color like this.

It turned to indigo. The indigo closed in and became black, but not a pure black, a black with reds and purples in it. The walls turned white again, the harsh white of artificial light. Eventually the sky got completely and totally black, black velvet, the kind that people paint pictures of snarling tigers, bleeding Jesuses and Elvis Presley on.

The stars came out and it was over. The twinkling lights gave the sky depth and spoiled the illusion. It was just a sky again filled with orbiting and spinning bodies. I left the skyviewer with the clear, pure feeling of having had an all-natural mind-altering experience.

The lights were on in Ci's kitchen and I went in. She was cutting up carrots and throwing them in a pot. Como was curled in a chair purring. "Well?" Ci asked.

"It was beautiful," I said.

"You've never seen colors like that before anywhere, have you?"

"No."

"The mind-altering, ecstatic experience—that's what some people live for."

"I hope that's not what Lonnie died for," I said.

Ci smiled, picked Como up and rested her chin on his head. "Death?" she asked. "What's death anyway, but a necessary transition, the ultimate altered state."

14

The next morning I made myself a Red Zinger when I got
to the office and tried not to listen while Anna and Brink
argued about what they wanted for breakfast. Brink
wanted an Egg McMuffin while Anna was leaning toward
a cinnamon raisin bagel. Since it was ten o'clock it seemed
like the breakfast issue should have been settled before
now. I shut my door, opened the *New Mexican* and caught
up on the Santa Fe crime scene. The City Different is a
mecca for artists, rip-off and otherwise. I went first to the
"Police Notes," where I found this: "A New York man and
his 31-year-old daughter traveling through the area got in
an argument in a Santa Fe restaurant Monday. The man
reportedly gave his daughter $50 and told her to 'hit the
road.' She did and has not been seen since."

The "Police Notes" are the minor crimes: the robberies,
the threats and arguments where no one gets hurt. When
rapes, beatings and murders are involved the stories move
onto page one, at least for a little while. Lonnie's death had

had its brief moment on the front page and now it was out of the newspaper altogether, unsolved, uninvestigated by anyone but me. I'd been talking to everyone who'd been connected with her, except that her two best friends were Jamie and Tim and I hadn't talked to them yet. I picked up the phone and dialed the number. Tim answered, Jamie was in her studio making pots. He told me he was giving a poetry reading that night and I agreed to come.

I took the shorter route to Dolendo and didn't see any *peregrinos* along the way. I-25 is the pilgrim path. It had been a while since I'd been to a poetry reading—about fifteen years. Tim's used to be raucous affairs with his friends drinking and cheering him on, making the Irish connection between words and drink. In San Miguel they had readings all the time. Except for MGM epics at the movie theater and the revolving bed antics of the gringos, there wasn't much else going on. The readings were never held on Monday nights, however, because Alcoholics Anonymous met then and too many of the writers in town were members.

This reading was to be at Babe's on Canyon Road, a bar and restaurant filled with plants. On Tuesday nights they encouraged anyone who wanted to to perform. No doubt Tim had something to say about life and death, but I wasn't expecting it to be raucous—sober and sad would be more like it. You feel an obligation to be happy in New Mexico with nothing around you but space and beauty and sunshine. If you can't feel good in such a beautiful place, then where can you? When you're down it's easy to sink into a dark pit, like an underground parking lot that's all the darker in contrast to the light; you can't help but hate yourself for falling in. Where it's gray all the time, you have gray ups and cloudy downs, but here there's light and there's dark, not much in between.

I turned at the Adobe of God and went up the rutted

road past the cemetery, wishing the Darmers had buried Lonnie in there the way people who died prematurely used to be buried under a tombstone shaped like a tree stump with the limbs cut off, the symbol of someone who died young. Anyone who went by it would know right away that the life had been short and the death sad.

Foxy Lady came out to meet me in the Malones' driveway wagging her long, red tail. "Hey, Foxy," I said. She'd miss not having her own cemetery to root around in in Ohio. As Tim said, living here was like being in the middle of a religious experience. I could see why you might not want to do it all the time. I could also see the appeal of a house in the green and gray Midwest (for a while anyway), but you wouldn't want to give Dolendo up forever either. They were renting, after all, not selling. As Foxy and I walked toward the door, I heard Tim and Jamie yelling at each other with that instinct for the throat that comes from long years of marriage.

"You're a fucking stone wall," yelled Jamie.

"You're paranoid," answered Tim.

I pounded on the door and listened to what sounded like embarrassed silence from the other side. Foxy Lady wagged her tail. When Jamie opened the door her expression was calm, as if she'd taken a hand and wiped the angry away. "Good to see you, Neil. Come on in."

Red mud had gotten stuck in the cleats of my running shoes and some of it fell out in clumps on the newly sanded and polyurethaned floor, unwelcome as roaches in Jamie's immaculately renovated house.

"Neil," she said, "would you mind? We always take our shoes off now that we have the new floors. I let people wear theirs at the party because there were so many people it would have been impossible to keep track of the shoes, but now I'm asking everybody to take them off."

I sat down on a bench, undid my laces and dropped my

shoes to the floor next to a pile of boots and assorted foot-gear, near a pair of Adidas running shoes even muddier than mine.

Jamie and I padded toward the kitchen across a floor whose hard, slick finish reminded me of proms and basket-ball games, corsages and sweat. "How 'bout a soda?" asked Jamie. "We don't keep hard stuff in the house anymore."

"Okay."

"Cream? Raspberry?"

"Cream."

Jamie took two out of the refrigerator, twisted the caps off and we sat down to drink them. Her hair fell across her face as she leaned over to sip at her soda. "Neil, I . . . um . . . I have a confession to make," she said. I waited. "I was the trickster."

"The trickster?"

"You know, Tricky Dick at Rick's party. I escorted you to the door."

"That was you? I didn't recognize the voice."

"Stop the Ugly," she said in a jowly Nixon mumble.

"I hope you will stop it, Jamie. That building sucks."

"We're trying," she sighed, "but it's not easy. I hear you went to see Ci."

"She told you?"

"Yeah. She doesn't want you investigating Lonnie's death. The investigation is holding the spirit on the earth plane, keeping it from moving into the light, Ci says."

"She would."

Jamie brushed her hair back. "Why are you doing it, Neil? Isn't that up to the police?"

"It should be, but they're not doing shit. The Darmers believe she was murdered, and they hired me to look into it."

"Who would murder Lonnie? Why would anybody mur-der Lonnie?"

"I don't know yet."

Tim appeared at the far side of the living room and walked across the floor in his stocking feet. His hair, charged with something—static electricity, maybe—buzzed around his head. "Neil, darlin'." He put his arm around me and gave me a charge.

"Timito," I replied.

"Timber," the unspoken third voice said, "Baloney, Maloney." Tim heard it, so did I, but Jamie wasn't listening. "I think we should get going," he said, staring at the far side of the kitchen with vacant newborn's eyes.

"What's the rush?" Jamie asked. "We've got time to finish our sodas."

"Take them with you. Let's go. Did you bring your car, Neil?"

"Not my car, the rental. Mine hasn't been fixed yet."

"Was I right, was it the carburetor?"

"You were right."

"Are you coming back here after the reading?" He was speaking to me but staring at the empty place near the microwave where he, Lonnie and I had stood.

"No."

"Then we'll be needin' two cars. Listen, Jamie, why don't I drive in with Neil, show her where Babe's is?" I knew where Babe's was, but that didn't seem to be the point.

Jamie may have known it too, but she said, "All right."

I was the first one onto the wooden floor, took a few running steps for momentum and slid over the gym finish in my stocking feet. I made it all the way across the living room in one long glide and got to the pile of shoes before anyone else did. "Your shoes, darlin'." I picked up the muddy Adidases and handed them to Tim, turning them over in my hand and noticing as I did the Vs that were embedded in the soles. If I'd gone into the bathroom I probably would have found the toilet seat up, too. Tim wasn't the tidiest guy in the world. "Your shoes look like they're flying south," I said.

"Huh?" replied Tim.

"The Vs," I showed him. "Like flying birds."

"Oh, yeah," said Tim.

"So?" Jamie asked, her eyes meeting mine over the shoes.

"So," I said. "Let's get out of here."

She grabbed a pair of loafers out of the pile and stepped into them. Foxy Lady, picking up on these not so subtle clues from the human side, went to the door and wagged her long, red tail. "I think we should leave Foxy in tonight," said Jamie.

"Out," replied Tim.

"In," said Jamie, pushing Foxy aside as we went out the door to our respective automobiles.

Jamie got her clutch engaged and her Toyota in gear faster than I was able to move the knob on the legger from P to D. She sped out of the driveway, leaving us in the mud. "Seems to be in a hurry," I said.

"A hurry to get away from me," replied Tim. He didn't say anything else so I watched the moon come up behind a mesa and spotlight the lonesome highway as I drove. It wasn't quite full yet and a little lopsided, but big enough to make coyotes howl and bright enough to hide the stars. Tim didn't speak until we reached the bridge and Jamie's distant taillights had gotten red and tiny as coyote eyes. "Don't ever get married again," were his words.

"I thought you two were happy if anybody was."

"Sometimes we are, sometimes we're not. It's been the pits lately."

"Is the move the problem?"

"Who the fuck knows what's the problem. Have you got a cigarette?"

"In my purse. You did say you quit, didn't you?"

"This doesn't count; it's yours. If I don't buy 'em and I don't smoke in the house where Jamie can smell it, then I'm not really smoking. See?" He fumbled around in my purse until he found the Marlboros. "You want one?" he asked.

"Why not?" I buy them, I smoke them. I'll admit it. He lit two cigarettes and passed one to me. "Lonnie and I had a heart to heart when we made this drive after your party," I told him since I didn't have anybody else to tell. "She asked me if I had slept with Rick; I told her I had but it was fifteen years ago."

"You, too? What do women see in that guy anyway?"

"Who knows? It was anybody and everybody back then. It only happened once."

"Did it bother Lonnie?"

"A little, but the fact that Rick is marrying Marci Coyle bothered her a whole lot more." I knocked the ash from my cigarette. "You know her parents don't think she killed herself."

"Neither do I."

"Then what do you think happened?"

"Rick killed her." Tim sucked in smoke, savoring every carcinogenic puff.

"How?" I asked, wondering what Tim knew about carotid sleepers and dangerous sexual practices. It didn't seem like something a long-married couple would do.

"He lied and cheated and broke her heart. That's why she took Valium and went to the ruins. For some reason I've never been able to understand, she was crazy about that jerk." Rick was rotten enough to be a good object for guilt projection. It was easy to say he was a scumbag and blame him for Lonnie's death, but the fact that *we* hadn't saved Lonnie didn't automatically make *him* guilty even if he did have a lousy alibi. Projection was emotionally satisfying, but it wasn't evidence and it wasn't admissible in a court of law.

"The Darmers have hired me to look into Lonnie's death," I said. "It probably makes you feel better to accuse Rick of killing Lonnie, but I need facts. There were eight hours between the time she left me and the time she was found dead. I still don't know where she went and who she saw." And none of her friends were admitting anything yet.

"Why don't you ask Rick?"

"I did. He says he didn't see her."

"Says. That's the key word." He ground the cigarette out in the ashtray, picked up my purse and began looking for another. "You've got everything else in here, how come you're not carrying condoms?"

"I don't carry condoms."

"Maybe you should. Sex has gotten dangerous; you never know when you'll be overcome by desire."

"When that happens these days, it's the Kid."

"Gettin' in deep, are you?"

"Not that deep," I said.

He continued searching through the purse. "I don't see a gun in here either."

"Why would I want to carry a gun?"

"If you're chasing a murderer, you ought to be armed."

"I'm armed with my brain," I said tapping my head.

"Oh, that. Well, from what I've seen in the war between smarts and guns, brains haven't won yet."

"Listen, Tim, I'm asking everybody else who knew Lonnie this, and I'm going to ask you. Did you see her or talk to her again that night?"

"No. The last time I saw her and ever will see her was when she left with you."

"Did you come to her house later?"

"No."

There was a pause while I put my own cigarette out. Tim filled the void. "I'm not lying, Neil. You ought to know me better than that." Maybe, but like I said, when it comes to someone else's husband there's always a far side to them you'll never know. I knew him well enough to think he wouldn't murder, but I also knew that murder isn't the only way to be responsible for someone's death.

We'd reached the Old Pecos Trail turnoff. A car came over the hill as I left I-25 and its headlights hit Tim smack in the face. I looked at his blinking newborn's eyes, thought about how well I knew him, and that not lying isn't the same as telling the whole truth. But it was time to move on to the next question. "Lonnie also told me she had proof that Jorge Mondragon had been paid off to approve the Ugly Building. Did she ever talk to you about that?"

"Yeah, she told me, but she didn't tell me what the proof was."

"Or where it was?"

"No."

"I'd kind of like to get in her house again," I said. "Probably whatever she had is long gone, but I want to take a good look just to be sure."

"You can have my key."

"You have one?"

"After my business went belly up, I used to go over there and hang out when Lonnie was at work and I needed to get out of my house. You get tired of sitting around your own place day after day looking at space, poking around in your subconscious. That's what I do, you know. It gets old and sometimes I need a change, a room with no view. But I'm not the only one who had a key to Lonnie's. There's Rick for starters. There's Ci." Tim took a key ring out of a pocket and took Lonnie's key off.

"You want it back when I'm done?" I asked him.

"What for?" he said.

15

It was amateur night at Babe's. The amateurs had brought their claques along; Jamie and I were Tim's. By the time we all got there she was again her calm self, as if she'd driven her anger away on the road over—you can do that on the lonesome highway.

A game I like to play when I go out in Santa Fe is guessing who's an artist and who wants to be mistaken for one, who's a pauper and who's a patron, who's from L.A. and who's from Texas. The first amateur to perform looked like an L.A. native to me. He had a table full of fans dressed in black who cheered him loudly. Maybe amateur night at Babe's was the equivalent of the Taos ugly truck contest with first going to worst. If that were the case I'd give it to this guy without even seeing anyone else. I didn't think it was possible to get any worse than him. It was a minimalist act; he stood on the small stage, dressed in black, smiling at his cheering friends and holding a boom box, also black. He put a wastepaper basket (black) over his head and tried to play something on the boom box, but he couldn't find the right buttons because he had a wastepaper basket over his head.

The claques tended to get up and leave after their amateur had performed—with good reason. There was a folk singer, a saxophonist, a storyteller, a guy who created a painting right before our eyes by throwing paint at a cringing canvas. By the time it was Tim's turn, there weren't many of us left. It's a lonely life being a poet.

He read poems about love, Foxy Lady and the view from Dolendo. And then he said, "This poem is dedicated to my friend Lonnie Darmer who died suddenly last week."

ONLY ALWAYS

Only in moments
    when the party conversation lags
    in predawn flashes of blind loss
    as day perfects itself from light

Only during queasy days between seasons
    witnessed rare places like mountaintops
    well-achieved deserts, at kitchen sinks
    driving, mating, in every automatic act

Only in the throes of distinction
    wrenched from that second place
    tucked between soul and the bone
    as we grudgingly separate from sky

Only at moments when purpose peeks
    from between the folds of a task
    as the one true stranger
    whispers along the blood: Live

Only there, Only always, Only now
    am I allowed to freely grieve you

"That was beautiful, darling," Jamie said when Tim was finished.

"I liked it, too," said I.

"I hope you weren't disappointed that more people didn't stay," Jamie added.

"No. That poem was for us, not them."

We paid our bill and went outside where the lopsided moon hung on over Canyon Road. A jet had passed by earlier, leaving a long trail that stretched out and notched like silver vertebrae beneath the moon. We walked to our cars and said good-bye. Tim and Jamie, who'd become a couple again, drove back to Dolendo in the Toyota.

I, who had rarely been part of a couple, went over to the West Side alone. I bumped down Lonnie's rutted driveway, parked and climbed the stoop where the cat had been found and the Vs had been imprinted between the snow's fall and melt, Vs that were probably put there by one of my friends, that had been seen by no one but me, that existed like certain colors only in my mind. Tim's key turned easily in the lock, no cats leapt out when I opened the door; they'd gone to Roswell with Bunny and Arthur, where they'd be safe. Sooner or later the Darmers would have to clear all the stuff out of here and take it back to the flea market. It made no sense for them to pay rent on a place that wasn't used, but if I told them that keeping the place exactly as it was would help the investigation, they'd do it forever. Everything was as it had been, only neater. The drawer that once held the journal contained nothing, the R. C. Gorman print was on the wall, the refrigerator was clean and empty, the toilet seat was down. I suspected that if Lonnie had had any evidence to incriminate Jorge Mondragon, Marci Coyle and/or anybody else, somebody had been here already and taken it, but I searched anyway. I looked in the drawers and in the closets, the books on the bookcases, the boxes of food left on the shelves. I looked under the pillows and under the bed, behind the pictures on the walls, the photographs on the bureau. I looked for hidden compartments, but found nothing. I went into the studio. The screens were on the windows, the hammock on its hooks, the spray cans on the card table. There was nothing hidden or incriminating to be found here, either. What I needed to do next was get outside, try to get into Lonnie's mind and follow her steps, enter the vacuum she had left behind. Where had she gone and why? She'd been here and ended up there—dead. I still didn't know what had happened in between. Lonnie, Lonnie, Lonnie, I thought, who should you have been warned about? I had brought her sweater with me, intending to leave it in the closet, but I put it on instead. Then I picked up a can and left the house, locking the door behind me, even though everybody who wanted to get in probably already had a key and anyone who didn't have their own could have easily used their husband's or lover's.

Lonnie had taken off into the shadows behind the main house, but the houses were so close here that in a few minutes you could cover most of the neighborhood if a dog, fence or wall didn't get in the way. It seemed a little early to go snooping around backyards, so I decided to take a walk instead, wait for the dogs to settle down and the neighbors to go to sleep. Besides, I had something I wanted to say. I walked down the hard-packed driveway that would soon be turning to red New Mexico mud and when I got to Miranda I turned right and headed for town. There were street lamps here and there, shedding just enough light to make the darkness seem darker. Miranda had been a street long before there were automobiles and it was so narrow in places only one car could get through. When you drove up to one of the bent-elbow corners you had to stop and hold your breath and hope you wouldn't meet someone coming around the bend, or beep your horn, but that lacked guts, and besides you'd be honking into somebody's bedroom window. In other spots Miranda was wide enough that two cars could pass each other—if one of them pulled up on the sidewalk—but you couldn't do that if cars were already parked there. When anybody entertained here, all the neighbors knew about it—they could hear the noise and the guests' cars would be scattered all over the street. It was close to eleven and it was relatively quiet considering there was an almost full moon. There were few cars parked on the street and not that many passed me, either. When they did, I had to look away because the light hurt my eyes.

I walked down a narrow strip of sidewalk next to a wall the height of my head. Suddenly a wail came from beyond that wall, disembodied like the screams I heard or dreamed the night Lonnie died. Only those screams were full of anger; this moan was thick with pain. It was one of those cries that comes out of the night, stabs you with primal fear and sinks back in, a cry with an inhuman dimension to it. There was another wail but from a more confident voice, the victor, the victim. A cat leapt up and landed surefooted on top of the wall. It walked along next to me for a minute curling its tail. There was a vicious yowl from behind the wall and the cat—the victim—jumped down and ran away. It was longhaired, black with a large white spot at the back of its neck.

I kept on walking and at the end of Miranda stepped onto brightly lit Alcazar and crossed the bridge over the Santa Fe River, noticing the sliver of black water that trickled through. In some places this body of water would be called a stream, in some places it wouldn't be noticed enough to be called anything, but it was water and it moved and if you followed it long enough it would lead you to the Rio Grande, to Texas and out to sea. I walked down Alcazar past a Dunkin' Donuts that must have gotten built long before there was an HPB. I passed Climb High Hiking Gear and Sunshine Natural Foods and turned onto Paloma. On Alcazar the lights were a high, even canopy like rain-forest trees. Paloma was more like Miranda, the lights were scattered and lonely. There was nothing to illuminate here anyway but a wall—gray, slapped-together, ugly. Lonnie's graffiti had been painted over and, for the moment at least, the wall presented a uniform surface of gray, too uniform to suit me. I walked up close, took a look down the street—empty. At the state office building across the way the windows were blank. All alone on Paloma, I removed the top of the can, pressed down hard on the nozzle and sprayed in large, ten-mile orange letters, a four-letter word. "You're ugly," I said, "ugly, ugly, ugly." I wasn't as fast or as skilled as Lonnie, but I think she would have been proud.

As I stepped back to admire my work something flashed. A blinking blue light came out of nowhere, around the corner and down the street. "Shit," I said. The car's headlights turned toward the wall and spotlighted me with a can of spray paint in hand and no place to hide it or me. The wall was too high to jump over, too strong to knock down, and there wasn't any gate through it. The unmarked car stopped and someone opened the door and stepped out, leaving the blue light flashing on the dashboard. Like the car, he was in civilian camouflage, but I recognized him anyway. He had an overly developed upper body, short legs, a macho walk. His name was Detective Michael Railback.

"Ms. Hamel." His smile expanded to suit the—for him—happy occasion, finding me at the crime scene with a dripping paint can in my hand. "What a pleasure to see you again."

"The pleasure is all yours."

"What brings you out tonight?" A rhetorical question.

"I'd like to see that can you've got there." I handed it over. He was prepared with a plastic bag that he opened up and dropped the can in. "Evidence," he said.

I said nothing. What was there to say?

"We've been getting a lot of complaints about people defacing this wall. We've been watching for 'em and we all take a drive by here when we're downtown. Every time someone paints 'ugly' on there, somebody else has to come by and paint it over. Makes a lot of work for the painters. Gets to be expensive, too. When the damage costs more than a thousand to repair, it's a felony." He shook his head slowly while he watched me.

It's not advisable for an attorney to be caught in a felonious act holding the smoking gun. It could well be the end of a career . . . or a living. "A thousand dollars?" I said. "It's not going to cost anybody a thousand dollars to paint over *that.*"

"It could. You might have to paint the whole wall to get it right. People are fussy about their walls and their paint jobs in Santa Fe." He walked up to my hastily sprayed-on UGLY and looked it over carefully, analyzing the thickness of the paint, the size of the letters, the balancing and articulation of the word. "But on the other hand if it's less than a thousand dollars' damage, it's a misdemeanor, not the kind of thing anybody'd form a task force over, not the kind of crime a DA's gonna be calling me up and harassing me about either. I guess now I've seen it up close, it don't look like no thousand dollars to me. So I'm gonna let you go, but remember, I got this." He held up the Baggie-enclosed spray can with my prints all over it. "And I sure hate having the DA on my case. I sure hate having anyone on my case. You call them off, I'll let you off. Got it?"

"Yeah, I got it." Like I said, it's a city where they don't take crime seriously. Sometimes that works for you, sometimes it doesn't.

He got back in his unmarked car, turned off the annoying blinking light and leaned out the window. "Give you a ride somewhere?" he asked.

"No," I replied.

He took off and I walked back down Alcazar wondering how I'd been so stupid as to get caught spraying paint on a wall and how Railback had been so lucky as to catch me doing it, wondering how deeply involved he was in all this, if he'd been watching Lonnie's house or tailing me, if his failure to investigate had been due to stupidity, laziness or plain old greed. If I got Dennis and the Darmers off Railback's case no one would help me solve Lonnie's death, but no one had helped me anyway. I was back where I'd started from and where I'd always been—having to solve it myself.

A low rider with a chain-link steering wheel and a pair of signature fuzzy dice hanging from the mirror cruised down Alcazar. The back of the car was hanging so low it scraped the pavement and shot off sparks. The driver hunkered behind the wheel and gave me a look that said he'd come back and soon; so I cut across the Santa Fe River and turned down Miranda before he did. It was quiet here now, even the dogs had shut up. I listened to my footsteps on the pavement, hurried under the lights, raced across the shadows, eased around the bends in the street. There were no vehicles pulled up on the sidewalk, all the guests on Miranda had gone home. A car came around a corner suddenly and I found myself staring into the headlights, widening circles of light, like the ripples stones make when they're dropped in the river. I was blinded to everything but the light, although the driver could see me clearly—my running shoes, my jeans, the pissed-off look on my face. The car continued on and so did I, down the narrow sidewalks where you brushed adobe from walls.

I turned down Lonnie's driveway, walking toward my car and blinking away the light. There was a dark spot on the hood of the white rent-a-Ford, one of those black holes you see after looking at light, only as I got closer I realized it was a cat. Its back was to me, the legs and tail spread out over the hood. Cats like to crawl onto cars and sleep on top of the warm engine—you find their paw prints all over your vehicle in the morning. I doubted if the engine would still be warm, but maybe the cat was sleeping too soundly to notice. "Get down, cat," I said. There was no response. "Get down," I said again. The animal didn't budge. Starting the engine would get him off, I figured, and if that didn't do it, moving the car would. I got out my keys, walked up close and took a look. The cat was longhaired, black with a white spot on the back of its neck, the same one I'd seen coming over the wall. There was a stain under the body spreading across the hood, a stain that had once been red but was turning black. The cat didn't move now and it would never move again. I grabbed its legs and flipped it over. The stomach had been split open with surgical precision from crotch to throat, and its guts spilled all over the hood.

16

I let myself into Lonnie's, locked the door behind me and sat down on the overstuffed sofa for a long moment. Then I went in the kitchen and found a garbage bag. I took the bag outside, picked the cat up by its legs and put it in, trying not to gag or throw up or touch the dead animal any more than I had to. Next I got a pail of water and a scrub brush, poured the water over the hood and scrubbed the guts off. I put the bag in the trunk and drove to the place where I'd seen the cat come over the wall, hoping no kids lived there. No kid wants to have someone knock on the door and tell them their pet is dead. Of all the bad things that can happen to a child, losing a pet has to be one of the worst. They'd probably know by the sound of the knock that something terrible had happened, but it's better to know than to wait day after day for an animal that never comes back. Waiting is a virus that saps your energy and kills you inch by inch.

I pulled up onto the sidewalk, leaving the bag in the

trunk, thinking that whoever the cat belonged to might not want to see it, then got out of the car, walked around to the gate and pulled at the string sticking through. A bell rang somewhere and a dog barked a couple of times, the deep bark of a large, secure pet.

"Be quiet, Blackie," a woman's voice called in musical English. "I'm coming."

She opened the gate and stood before me, holding onto the dog by a short leash, backlit by a porch light, a tiny gnarled being, more spirit than person, bent over into the shape of the curled-up shrimp she'd been ninety or so years ago. Her eyes were large and unnaturally bright, her face wrinkled like a dried apricot. She might not have been much older than Pete Vigil, but she'd crossed a frontier and entered the no-man's-land between life and death. I didn't enjoy being the one to tell her that her cat had gone first and how it had gotten there, or that, in a way, I had been responsible. The dog, a large, black chow with its tail curled and its ears pointed, watched me warily.

"Yes?" she asked, looking up with luminous eyes.

"I'm sorry," I said. "I hope I didn't wake you."

"I'm too old to sleep."

"I left my car down the street at Lonnie Darmer's and . . ."

"You were a friend of hers?"

"Yes."

"She's dead."

"I know."

"She was a good girl, wasn't she, Blackie? She always asked me if I wanted something when she went to the store. She's with the angels now."

"I took a walk and when I got back I found a dead cat on my car," I said.

"What did it look like?"

"Longhaired, black, with a white spot on the back of its

neck. I saw it come over your wall earlier."

"That's Manolo. I heard him scream before and I knew something bad was happening to him. How did he die?"

"He was . . . cut open."

"*Dios mio!* Those bad boys in this neighborhood. You never know what they will do next. They get the killing disease and they kill anything: cats, dogs, themselves, each other, their own mothers and sisters even." She shook her head and wisps of white hair fell loose. "That's why I don't let you go out, Blackie, but you can't keep a cat home; they go over the wall."

"There's a cute blond boy named Dolby who lives near here. Do you know him?"

"Dolby? He doesn't live here. I would know him if he did."

"I have the cat in my car, if you want to bury it."

"Where do you live?"

"Albuquerque."

"You could do something for me and leave him beside the highway on your way home. Find a good place for my Manolo. The birds will eat his body, but the angels will take his spirit." She wasn't exactly sentimental about death, but maybe she was close enough to know something the rest of us didn't. "Your friend, Lonnie, liked cats. She'll be happy to have Manolo in heaven with her. She talks to me sometimes."

"What does she say?"

"She likes it there."

"Did she tell you how she died?"

"She went to sleep. She says she's waiting for me. It won't be long now, I can tell you that. I'm ready. Could you help me back to the house before you go?"

"Of course." Her hand clutched my arm like a claw as I led her across the yard. Blackie followed, still watching me. When we got to the door, the woman released her grip. Her face was tilted toward the porch light, her eyes supernaturally large and luminous. I waved my hand in front of them, but nothing blinked, moved or registered. "Do you want me to open the door for you? Help you in?" I asked.

"Oh, no," she said. "I can do that. Find my Manolo a good place."

"I will," I said.

I stopped when I got to the top of La Bajada, pulled the car off the road, climbed a knoll and dumped Manolo out of the garbage bag. It seemed as good a place as any to join the ranks of those who've turned to bone beside the highway. Once you're dead, it probably won't make a shitload of difference to you where you end up or how you end up, but I'd like a witness, anyway, someone to know for sure that I'm gone and where the remnants are. *"Adios,* Manolo," I said. *"Vaya con dios."*

The highway, some people say, is the best place to think. As I drove home to Albuquerque I thought about murderers and ways to catch them. One way is to track down witnesses to the crime. There are always two at least—the victim and the killer—but the victim can't talk and the killer won't. Another way is to find incriminating evidence, but the evidence I had gathered so far existed either in my mind or in an envelope in Detective Railback's desk. It looked like I might have happened upon the third and least desirable method—to get the killer to come to you. If I was going to solve this crime, that was one way to do it. The killer seemed willing enough to oblige. Girls don't go out to ruins alone to die, cats don't climb up on cars and gut themselves. Lonnie had found a cat on her stoop, Lonnie was dead. I'd found one on my car, I could very well be next. I'd been conducting an investigation and, for all anybody knew, had incriminating evidence by now. I also fit the victim profile: an independent, white female in her thirties who had a past, who lived alone, who'd written UGLY on the wall. I needed protection, but didn't know where I'd find it. Detective Railback wasn't likely to provide me with an armed guard. The Kid would tell me to get out of the murder business and go back to deeds and divorces. Where he came from they had no illusions about what life is worth on the open market, on any market.

I passed Budaghers, the exit that goes nowhere, and around the time I reached San Felipe the radio offered a solution, one of those disembodied voices that appears to answer your prayers. When the listener is ready, the voice speaks. This one came from KJOY-FM. "Ladies, if you're looking for a firearm for personal protection, consult Ron Peterson Guns." I made a note to do just that tomorrow.

There were still a few *peregrinos* beside the highway even though it was after midnight. I've always wondered whether someone picks them up and takes them home to sleep in their beds and return in the morning or if they walk all night. The ones I saw weren't carrying any bedding. The highway didn't seem like a safe place to be after midnight, even for a man. Maybe they carried personal protection, too.

When I got back to La Vista I locked up tight and said good night to the mantel before I went to bed. The rose was floating in its forever red solution, the vertebrae were zeros surrounded by bone. The Kid leaned against a wall smiling. I kissed his picture, got into bed, watched the light crawl across the ceiling and dreamed about cats: bloody cats, screeching cats, clinging cats, cats that were out and wanted to get in, cats that had been in and climbed out.

I woke early and drove to work in the dawn's flamingo glow looking for the combination of sun and wall that would transform Lead to Gold; I didn't find it. At Baja Tacos I got a Red Zinger and an egg burrito with extra chile to go, hoping the chile would light my fire. The law offices of Hamel and Harrison have wrought iron over the windows that might pass for decorative grillwork, but it's really bars. I like to know that what I find in the morning will be what I left behind at night. Bars keep *them* out, us in. We also have Anna to screen the undesirables. She has an image of the kind of client Hamel and Harrison ought to represent. Unfortunately it bears little resemblance to the kinds of clients who ask us to represent them. I was the only car in the driveway, but that's what I expected so early in the day. I fumbled in my purse for my key chain, unlocked a couple of locks, let myself in, sat down at my desk and ate the burrito. The chiles weren't as hot as those little green zingers they eat for breakfast in Central America. They pop those in their mouths and onto their tongues because if your lips ever touched one they would burn and blister. But the burrito was hot enough to open my eyes and ready me to face the day. It was still early to be making calls, but there was one person I knew who was ambitious, hardworking and conscientious enough to be in, Dennis Quinlan, the DA for Santa Fe County.

He answered his own phone. "Dennis," I said, "you're in early."

"Not for me, but I thought you had your own practice so you didn't have to get to work early."

"I thought so, too."

"I don't have anything new on the Darmer case, I'm sorry to say."

"That's why I'm calling. I ran into Railback yesterday and I think it would be better if you left him alone. Pushing is only making him hostile. It's not helping me and it'll cause problems for you down the road." I'd said I'd do it; it was done.

"In all honesty, Neil, it does look like a bad combination of substances, an accident or a suicide." To him maybe.

"Thanks for your help, Dennis."

"Glad to do it," he answered with what sounded like a sigh of relief, one less problem for an overworked public servant.

Since I'd been spending so much time on the highway lately I had a lot of paperwork to catch up on. It was a good time; the phones weren't ringing, nobody was around. It would be interesting, anyway, to see what time Anna and Brink arrived for work. It surprised me when Anna showed up at nine fifteen and poked her moussed and pouffed head in my office. "You're here early," she said.

"I have a lot of paperwork to do."

"That's right. We haven't seen much of you lately. You haven't heard my dead lawyer joke yet, have you?"

"You're going to tell me a dead lawyer joke?"

"Yeah. You know how to tell the difference between a dead lawyer in the road and a dead armadillo?"

"The lawyer has tougher skin?"

"No. There are brake marks in front of the armadillo."

"Ha, ha. Close the door on your way out."

"Jeez," I heard her say as she shut the door. "What's the matter with her?"

By noon I'd done what I had to do and was left with a bottomed-out feeling that even green chile wouldn't lift, so I went out and took a ride around the Duke City. I stopped at Old Town, parked and walked through the narrow streets that tourists find so appealing and where you're not likely to see anyone who actually lives here. There was a wedding finishing up at the Adobe of God and the bride and groom were standing out front receiving guests. They were young and beautiful. She had naturally auburn hair and wore an ivory dress with some sort of embroidery that sparkled tastefully in the sun. They looked like they came from what my aunt Joan called a good family, the kind of family that directed their young toward a clearly defined goal, whose members stayed married, reproduced, spent holidays together; a family who never committed or was victimized by a crime, who didn't get addicted or murdered. I never believed people like that actually existed, but looking at this couple could almost convince me.

I left Old Town and drove over to 12th Street, the one area of Albuquerque that doesn't look like it. It has the kind of pastel Victorian bungalows with second stories and lace curtains in the windows that are endemic somewhere else, the Southeast maybe. I come here sometimes when I get the feeling my life is a desert, when the pastel and lace seem not sappy but snug, when I need to experience the opposite. White irises, lilacs and tulips were blooming all over people's yards. Fruit trees were the color of black raspberry ice cream and birds were lapping it up. I parked on Roma, went to Mary Fox Park and sat down under the wisteria arbor. This was a place women pushing babies in strollers came during the day to sit around and gossip. Would there ever be a place for me in a neighborhood like this? I wondered. In spite of welcoming spring with a reckless afternoon of unsheathed love, I hadn't gotten pregnant. Did I wish I were? Sometimes you get tired of thinking and planning, sometimes you feel like turning your fate over to a reckless act; careless love is as reckless an act as most people are capable of. But when you've done it and it's too late to change what you've done, you'd probably start wishing you hadn't. What would the Kid make of this neighborhood? I wondered. What would this neighborhood make of him? Would it find him young and greasy fingered? I got up, drove to Ron Peterson's pink-and-turquoise building on Central and bought myself a gun.

The person who sold it to me was a large, secure male with a diamond in his ear and a courtly manner. He was such a gentleman that he made me feel like a lady, a lady in need of protection.

The gun I bought was a Smith & Wesson LadySmith handgun, a .38, practical, yet elegant, matte deep blue, with a custom grip specially designed for the female hand. It cost about as much as repairing my car. I couldn't afford it, but, as the catalog said, it was "the answer to [my] special—and very contemporary—needs." I paid with plastic and walked out with the LadySmith in my purse. All it took was some credit and my signature on a paper stating that I wasn't a convicted felon and neither a marijuana nor a cocaine addict. If I'd had a holster I could have walked down the street with bullets in the gun. In the Land of Enchantment a loaded gun is legal as long as it is not concealed. You're not supposed to carry one in your purse, but the offense is only a misdemeanor, the equivalent of a traffic violation. You can keep a loaded gun in your house, however, and your car is considered your house here. Time is of the essence in matters of personal protection; an un-loaded gun is a waste of precious time. When I got in the legger, I put the bullets in my LadySmith.

I was sitting on my living room sofa examining it when the Kid showed up early for dinner.

"What are you doing with that, Chiquita?" he asked.

"I think Lonnie was murdered and I'm afraid the killer might be after me," I told him.

"Why would anybody murder her?"

I gave him the most logical explanation. "It could be because she found out someone had been paid off to ap-prove the Ugly Building."

"People kill for a building?" the Kid said.

"People kill for anything, people kill for the sake of kill-ing."

"Why don't you call the police?"

"I tried. Either they don't believe me, or they've been paid off, too."

"I have some money, Chiquita, if you need it."

It was simple where he came from: when you needed help from a public official, you paid them. Here that kind of corruption is available only to the seriously rich. "Thanks, Kid, but I think it would take a lot more money than you and I'd ever be able to scrape together."

"If you think someone wants to kill you, stop the investigation, go to Colorado or someplace till it's over," he said, even though he probably knew what my answer would be.

"I can't," I replied.

He shrugged. "I know you, Chiquita, I know how you are. You never stop, but when you carry a gun someone can use it on you."

"Probably no one will ever use it on anyone. It just makes me feel better to have it."

The Kid picked up the weapon and turned it over in his hand. "This is a *woman's* gun."

"I'm a woman. What do you know about guns anyway?"

"I know you should never have them in the house. Someone gets mad one minute, they do something like that . . ." He pointed the gun at me. "And they are sorry about it forever."

"Kid, that gun is loaded. Don't point it at me."

He put it down. "I don't like this in the house."

"It's not your house," I reminded him.

"I'm here, but I won't stay here with that gun."

Was he saying that he didn't trust me, himself or people in general? It's hard to tell sometimes what the Kid is thinking, but not hard at all to tell when he's made up his mind. He'd be out of here in two minutes once he'd decided to go. His past was Mexican, mysterious, overloaded with images of birds, flies and people. He grew up on the edge of the biggest slum in the Western world and had crossed a border illegally God knows how many times. I didn't know what violence and misery he'd seen and I probably never would; his eyes turned cloudy when the past was mentioned. Whatever had happened, his spirit had remained lighthearted, and I wouldn't want to mess that up.

"All right. I'll lock it in the car," I said.

He shrugged as if to imply that would do for now, but not forever. I took the gun out to the La Vista parking lot and locked it in the rent-a-Ford glove compartment. Considering the activity in that lot it could only be considered a temporary solution.

17

During the night spring turned to summer, for a little while anyway. When I left for work at nine thirty it was already eighty degrees, shirt-sleeve or, in some places, no-sleeve tattoo-baring weather. The Kid and I had made our peace about the gun, it wouldn't come into the house when he was there. I checked the glove compartment and found the LadySmith—my personal protection—in place. I rolled the windows down and waited for the air conditioner to kick in as I drove across town. I was kind of enjoying the sounds of the street so I kept the windows down and turned the air conditioner off.

When I got to the office Anna was trying to get rid of one of those people she thinks we shouldn't represent. You have to have a bigger income than Hamel and Harrison's to afford pro bono work, and that's what that guy looked like—someone who had big problems and couldn't afford to solve them. He had a scruffy way of dressing that said either deeply committed hippie or long-term homeless.

Hippie to me, hopeless to Anna. She was too young to know the difference between those who dressed that way out of necessity and those who did it by choice. Anna's revolving miniskirt wardrobe made *her* statement about materialism, buy cheap, buy often. The guy she was showing the door to was a medium-size Anglo. His hair was pulled into two ponytails and wrapped with leather thongs that had feathers sticking out. I'd seen his ugly truck parked on the street so I knew he wasn't entirely homeless. He had an income, too, selling bones at the flea market. It was the guy with a spiderweb tattoo, the Vietnam vet who might have a clue for me, or might only be an attempt on Pete Vigil's part to hold my attention—the bone man.

"I was hoping you'd show up," I said.

Anna's mouth puckered with distaste like she'd found something sour in the yogurt she was eating. "You know him?" she asked.

"We've met."

The bone man's hand reached out to take the door away from me. "Your secretary here don't want me around."

"It's a mistake," I said. "Don't leave. I need to talk to you." Damn you, Anna, I thought, glaring in her direction.

"She thinks maybe I got AIDS or somethin'."

"Come on into my office. We can talk there."

"I only came here because of Pete Vigil."

"I know."

"I just got one thing to say to you anyway." Anna watched this exchange silently, her spoon suspended in the yogurt container.

"What's that?"

"Guide Line."

"That's all?"

"That's it. Go out there this afternoon and you might find what you're lookin' for, if you're still lookin'. But me,

I'm outta here." His hand grabbed the door, pulled it open and slammed it on his way out.

"God damn it, Anna," I said. "Why weren't you civil to him? He has some information for me about Lonnie's death."

"Him? He's a bum."

"Bums see a lot, hear a lot. They make good observers, because nobody notices them." I heard the ugly truck's engine catch and rev up. The tailpipe rattled and coughed and, like he'd said, he was out of here. "He's not a bum, anyway. He works."

"Yeah? What does he do?"

"He deals in bones—antlers, skulls—at the flea market. People buy them for decoration, to make chandeliers and stuff."

"Were you gonna take your fee in bones?" she asked, finishing up the yogurt and throwing the empty carton at the trash.

"I wasn't going to represent him. He just came here to give me some information, that's all."

"Guide Line? Doesn't sound like much."

"Well, we'll see, won't we?"

I went into my office, shut the door and looked up Guide Line in the phone book. It was a tattoo parlor way out on Central SW, formerly known as Route 66. Probably on Nine Mile Hill where the seedy motels with dirty videos are. Nine Mile Hill sounds like the name of a battle to me, a battle with heavy casualties that nobody won. I was going out there this afternoon. I had other plans for this evening.

I sat at my desk drawing on a yellow legal pad. Yellow paper was one more depredation inflicted by attorneys on the embattled environment; we'd have to start buying white soon for recycling. As I drew Vs on my pad I thought about means, motive, opportunity, evidence, what I knew, what I didn't. If Lonnie had been killed in the ways Robert

Fitch suggested, everybody I'd talked to had the means—their fingers or the missing sleeping bag—and, considering the unverifiability of their alibis, they all had the opportunity, too. There were the usual motives, greed, revenge, jealousy, sex, but did any of the suspects have the heart full of malice necessary to commit cold-blooded murder? Of course there might not have been a murder. Lonnie's death could have been an accident, or a reckless or wanton act, a psychic or sexual experiment, say, that went too far, although the crime scene didn't show carelessness. It showed nothing with the possible exception of cold calculation. I considered evidence next, evidence only I had seen: a pattern of Vs on the stoop, a toilet seat left up, the signs possibly of a careless or emotional person. There were three crimes to consider: robbery, rape, murder. Intending to find out how many criminals, I picked up the telephone and dialed Jamie Malone. Maybe Tim hadn't been lying when he told me he didn't come to Lonnie's that night, but Jamie'd never been asked. I said I wanted to meet her at 7½ Miranda after work. She agreed, hesitated briefly and said, "I'm sorry, Neil, I should have called you."

Even though I spent the afternoon pushing papers around my desk I still felt like I'd been making left-hand turns all day into traffic. At four I went out to Nine Mile Hill to make some real-life turns. I said good-bye to Anna and told her to hold down the fort, which in my mind meant be civil to anyone who came in. She answered "yeah" like she might have gotten the message. The temperature had gone up to eighty-five and I left the windows in the legger down, drove out Lead and cut over to Tingley Drive. The water in the lagoon next to the Rio Grande was turquoise blue for some reason and sparkled in the sun. Usually it had the color and effervescence of mud. OBJECTS IN MIRROR ARE CLOSER THAN THEY APPEAR, the writing on my side-view mirror said, but the trucks here cruised so slowly they'd never catch up to me. Guys were fishing in the lagoon or standing on the banks admiring each other's cars, boom boxes and tattoos. I turned left at The Beach apartment complex, one of the more successful architectural statements around, got on Central, crossed the river and began to climb Nine Mile Hill. At the top there's a sign that says DANGEROUS CROSSWINDS and a spectacular view of the Duke City and the elephants resting behind it. Albuquerque isn't like one of those coastal cities that's part of a sprawl from Washington, D.C., to Maine. It's an inland, Western city; it begins, it ends and from Nine Mile Hill you can see it happening. There is city and beyond that nothing. On the way up I passed a billboard that said YOUR HIGH SCHOOL QUARTERBACK IS LEARNING NEW SIGNALS IN THE NAVY. A body shop displayed a dazzling yellow truck with orange flames licking the hood. The golden oldie station on the radio was playing some apocalyptic Doors song. Between the mobile home community and the snake garden I found Guide Line Tattoos in the Motel Nine. I parked the legger in the parking lot and left the windows open an inch so I wouldn't be stifled by dead air when I got back in. The combination tattoo parlor–motel was low, gray, ugly. It would have been invisible if it weren't for the large sign out front that advertised tattoos and a room for two for $12.95 with adult videos. The sign had movable letters, but they'd moved the wrong ones because today's feature was called *The Fine Art of Connilingus.* "Adult" was a misnomer; I didn't see any around, only teenage boys. Apparently they came here after school, if they went to school, to get tattooed and do their homework.

A guy with a prominent belly stood behind the desk. He wore a black cap on his head, probably to cover a bald spot. The hair that hung down from under the cap was grayish brown and stringy. Bare, beefy arms leaned over the counter advertising his artwork. Tattoos he'd gotten in his youth were expanding in middle age: serpents uncoiled, hearts broke, the web around his elbow stretched and tortured the insect trapped inside.

He watched and waited as I came through the door like maybe he was expecting someone else to share the $12.95. It couldn't happen very often that anyone came in here and asked for a single. As I probably didn't intend to get tattooed or watch dirty movies alone, I made him nervous. There was always the possibility that I was an undercover member of a vice squad or the mother of one of the teenage boys. I hate to think that I've gotten old enough to be the mother of a teenage boy, but I could be if I'd started early and they do around here.

"Whatta you want?" he asked.

"The man who sells bones at the flea market sent me."

"Chico." Someone he knew. That relaxed him a bit.

"Yeah." Chico sounded like as good a name as any for the bone man. "I'm Neil Hamel."

"Checker Martin."

"You and Chico have the same tattoo."

He looked at his bruised elbow. "So?"

"What does the fly in the web mean?"

"It means I killed a gook." A rite of passage in some circles.

"I guess that means Chico killed one, too."

"You got it."

"Where'd you get tattooed?"

"Da Nang, but we do 'em here now. Is that why Chico sent you? You want a tattoo?" He grinned.

"No, I'm looking for a killer."

"Yeah? Who got killed?"

"A woman in Santa Fe."

"What was her name?"

"Lonnie Darmer."

"You a cop?"

"No. She was a friend of mine."

He sized me up. I guess he didn't see whatever spelled cop in his mind, because he relaxed a little more, stretched his big arms, cracked his knuckles. "Didn't know her. Don't know why Chico thought I did or why he sent you here."

"We're both friends of Pete Vigil's."

"Don't know him either."

"Maybe you've tattooed a fly in someone's web."

"And if I did?"

"You could be sheltering a murderer."

"Well, a person who'd get a tattoo like that ain't the kind of person you'd want to snitch on, now is it? A person who's killed once might not think too hard about killing again. What goes on in my place is confidential anyway. That's why people come here." Checker Martin's eyes were flat and gray and had pinpoints for pupils. I doubted if there was any soul behind them or if they'd ever been the window to anything, but if so, that window was closed and boarded up now and he wasn't about to let me peek in. They weren't the kind of eyes you could bounce your own reflection off of, either. I tried looking into them, came up empty. He took evasive action anyway, slowly taking a toothpick from a box on the counter and slowly sticking it into his mouth. "Besides," he grinned once the toothpick was firmly implanted, "we get lovers here, not killers."

"You get many 'lovers' from Santa Fe? And any of them that do business with or buy bones from Chico?"

"I get 'em from all over. Hell, I don't ask what they do or where they're from."

A couple of boys wandered in taking a break between shows. "Hey, Checker," one of them said, "gimme some change for the soda machine." Too young to drink beer with his porn, the boy was tall and skinny with ripe pimples. He had a kind of unloved, unwashed aura, wore jeans and running shoes, fidgeted nervously while he waited for the change. Checker got up to get it. "Getting fat, Checker," the boy said. "Real fat."

"Son, when you got a stretch limo, you gotta build a garage to fit over it." The boy laughed, Checker laughed back.

I decided to watch today's feature to see if it had anything to tell me about this place and why I'd been sent here. Checker took my $12.95 and led me to a room where a sleazy red spread covered a bed whose springs had been flattened by the thumps of loveless screwing. There was a bedside table with a cheap lamp and a large TV. That was it for furniture. There wasn't even any velvet art on the walls. *The Fine Art of Connilingus* had an interesting beginning—for a porn film. A man and a woman were trying to turn another woman on. The older of the two women faced the camera and explained how. "Listen to the body," she said, reasonably enough, while she stroked the all too visible younger woman. The guy, who didn't get the part because he had a big brain, licked his lips, then began to demonstrate what he called "connilingus." There was a lot of attention lavished on one small section of one woman and she seemed to be getting genuinely turned on, but then a few more women entered the scene and it degenerated as porn films do—into a group grope with a lot of pointless shifting of positions and faked enthusiasm. It was stupid, laughable or boring depending on your mood—or your age. The Motel Nine had thin walls and I could hear the boys in the next room hooting while I was yawning, laughing as I was getting ready to leave. Maybe it was a question of sex, age and experience, or maybe we weren't watching the same thing.

I turned the video off and went out to the desk. "How'd you like it?" asked Checker Martin.

I shrugged. "Your basic dumb porn. Is that what the boys in the next room are watching?"

"Not exactly."

"What is it?"

"*Slasher*. You wouldn't want to see it."

"Why not?"

"It ain't the kind of video you'd like."

"How do you know?"

He looked at me with his pinpoint eyes. "You saying you want to see it?"

"Yeah."

"That'll be another $12.95." I handed over the money. "But don't say I didn't warn ya."

I went back to the sleazy room and started *Slasher* way behind the boys beyond the wall so their reactions were still out of sync with mine, but the reactions of boys like that would always be out of sync with mine. *Slasher* was stupid, but it wasn't laughable, and I guess you'd have to say it wasn't boring. It was a video that took a sick and ugly mind to make. I didn't watch the whole thing, but what I saw was as corrosive as lye burning a hole in my brain and my stomach, too. The odds had changed. In this case it was five men and one lone, naked woman who must have been beyond desperation to perform in this thing—if she was performing. The guys were bikers, she was supposed to be a groupie, I guess. It wasn't long before they got off their motorcycles and had her out in the woods somewhere. She had black leather cuffs around her wrists, ankles and neck attached to chains that stretched her across the ground. The bikers stood over her, jacked off and pissed on her naked body. They made their mark by carving their initials on her stomach and breasts and it got worse. The woman screamed and bled, the bikers laughed. There are such things as snuff films, where women are supposedly killed on camera. I had no way of knowing if this was one of those or not, but it was realistic enough to make me sick. A woman devalued, debased, defiled—snuffed—for sport. It was the way some people earned a living, and others spent their afternoons.

I yanked the video out. On my way past I tried the door to the boys' room, but the door was locked and they didn't offer to let me in. When I got to the desk I threw the video at Checker Martin. "Hey, don't blame me. I told you you weren't gonna like it," he said.

"You take money for this shit and from kids, too. I blame you."

"I got the right. It's a free country and I fought to keep it that way." Checker Martin's gray eyes did have an expression now—pissed off.

So was I. "Any sane person has an obligation to have nothing to do with this stuff."

"If they see it, then they don't have to do it."

It was an old and piss-poor argument. "Yeah, or they see it and they learn how."

I couldn't go back to work after that but it wasn't time to leave for Santa Fe either, so I drove around town thinking that I hadn't gotten a name but I might have gotten a motive, wondering what kind of a person would tattoo a spiderweb on their arm or watch snuff videos, wondering when sex got mixed up with hatred and violence. Thinking that there must have been a time and place when men and women were in better balance. At the ruins, maybe, five hundred years ago, where the women had their essential roles and the men theirs and whatever enemies they had were not each other. The only records anybody has of that time and place are abstract images scratched on stone, so nobody really knows for sure, but we can imagine and that's what people do imagine in New Mexico. Surrounded by beauty, it's not so hard to imagine harmony. When the ruins were inhabited the Anasazi were making the transition from hunter-gatherers to cultivators. As they settled down and began to grow corn, they stopped stalking and being stalked, and pushed danger beyond the circle around the fire. Now that we have the illusion of controlling the environment the boundaries of the circle have expanded, only the enemy has resurfaced within. Man was a hunter for millions of years before he settled down, maybe the imprint is too deep to go away. We also live in a culture where the message is always that you're not young enough, blond enough, rich enough, thin enough, fit enough, and the only way some people make themselves feel better is to make someone else feel worse. Statistics say there is a murder every twenty-five minutes in this country. Violence is as American as apple pie, predictable as spring, pervasive as pollen; a highly contagious virus, and those whose immune systems have been weakened are all too susceptible. You could blame it on too many people, too little space, but you can't call New Mexico overcrowded and violence has gotten the upper hand here, maybe everywhere. You couldn't stop it, you couldn't even move away from it, the best you could hope for was to protect yourself.

I checked to make sure the LadySmith was still in the glove compartment, turned down Coors Boulevard, cut across Gun Club Road, up Isleta, crossed Rio Bravo onto University and came out behind the airport. There is a spot back there where you go around a curve, come up an incline and suddenly you're surrounded by dunes. You can't see anything but sand and sky and a couple of tumbleweeds stuck on the dunes. I go there sometimes when I want to look at nothing.

I got on the interstate at Gibson, and passed an ornate black and chrome semi. The driver flashed his high beams when he saw I was a woman, alone. I stepped on the gas, put some distance between us, remembering that objects in the mirror are closer than they appear. The objects in the mirror were the usual collection of junkers and trucks. I didn't see any *peregrinos* in the city limits; they'd all walked further north by now. I did see a billboard that said IF YOU'RE THINKING OF COCAINE, CALL US and an ad for Ron Bell, who also sues uninsured motorists.

18

Jamie was in the driveway at 7½ waiting for me behind the wheel of the Toyota. She hadn't been able to let herself in the house because I had Tim's key. We got out of our respective cars, said hello and walked toward the door together. When we got to the stoop I said, "Jamie, I saw the cleat marks from Tim's running shoes in the snow right here the morning after Lonnie died. What I want to know is, Who was wearing them? Tim says it wasn't him."

"Why don't we go inside and talk about it?" she replied.

Some people think bad news can be made better by a cup of tea. Jamie found bags in the kitchen and boiled up some Emperor's Choice. I seemed to be the only one to notice that the emperor's bags had no tea in them. The drink was bland and pale as smoke. If I can't have taste in my tea, I'd at least like color. We sat down in the living room under the melancholy R. C. Gorman portrait and sipped at the hot water. Compared to Gorman's limp woman, Jamie seemed firm and solid. She sat up straight and brushed her hair back from her face. Jamie doesn't have hair like Tim's that reacts to every change of electricity or weather. Her hair hangs smooth and straight; when it's gone as far as she wants it to, it ends. She sighed, sipped at her choice and then she asked me, "What were you doing here that morning?"

"I spent the night."

"You did? Where?"

"In the studio."

"That explains it. I didn't realize you were here."

"I figured. Tell me about it." I'd known Jamie for fifteen years. Was I about to discover a far side to her that I didn't know? She had usually been calm, occasionally angry, always reliable—maybe *that* had taken its toll. She seemed willing enough, eager even, to talk, as if what she knew was a burden, a burden she was about to pass on to me.

"Tim and I had a fight after everybody left. We've been fighting a lot lately. This one was bad; I got into the white zinfandel at the party."

"What were you fighting about?" I asked, even though I probably knew already.

"Lonnie. What else? I was sick of watching her and Tim flirting. They've always been close, but it seemed to have gotten much worse lately. Tim's business failed, he was having trouble with his writing, Lonnie had broken up with Rick probably for the final time. They were crying on each other's shoulders and everybody knows where that leads. It was driving me crazy."

"You didn't let on."

"Not in front of anybody else, maybe; she was my best friend, he's my husband, what could I say? If I was even suspicious, he'd say I was paranoid. I'd blow up when Tim and I were alone, though, I couldn't help it."

Jealousy is the worst emotion; there's nothing ennobling or enlightening about it. It's a green-eyed monster. Like a parasite you pick up in Mexico, once you let it in it'll gnaw at your insides and swallow your guts until there's no you and a lot of him, a large worm that's gotten fat by eating you.

"I had to know what was going on before we left here," Jamie continued. "I didn't want to be stuck in Ohio with no support group and a husband who was in love with another woman. It's crazy, I know, but I was afraid Tim wanted to get me safely settled somewhere else and then find some excuse to come back here and be with Lonnie."

It was pretty crazy, but jealousy, like the full moon and certain substances, has a way of bringing out the craziness. I'd say it was more likely that Tim wanted to get them both to Ohio and away from Lonnie and his failed business here. "So what were you doing in Tim's shoes?" I asked.

Jamie's hair had fallen in front of her face again. She put down her empty teacup and brushed it away. "We took all the shoes out of the entryway for the party and threw them in the closet and they got mixed up. Tim had his Adidases on when he went out to look for Foxy Lady and he hadn't put them back in the pile, so I grabbed them and wore them. My feet are almost as big as his anyway. I took the Toyota and drove into town to confront Lonnie. Like I said, I'd been drinking."

"Couldn't you just have asked Tim?"

"Have you ever tried to talk to a man, Neil, I mean really talk to one about emotions?"

Had I ever tried to talk to anybody—male or female—about emotions? "Probably not," I said.

"It's the male disease. They can't talk about how they feel. I've tried to talk to Tim, but he wouldn't respond, not really. He'd always say it was nothing, but it didn't look or feel like nothing to me, so I came here. I saw Lonnie's car in the Club West parking lot on my way over and I figured you two had gone there."

"You didn't see Rick's car there, too, did you?"

"No. I had Tim's key so I came here and let myself in the house. I had no idea you were here. I went into the bedroom . . . and I . . ."

She hadn't confronted Lonnie, but she did the next best thing. "You took the journal?"

"Yeah. I was going to give it right back, but then . . . she died and there was no one to give it to."

"What about her parents?"

Jamie shook her head no. "You'll see why when you read it." She reached into her woven African bag, pulled the journal out, handed it to me.

I took it, but I didn't want to read it. "Just tell me one thing. Did it say that Rick was a violet lover or a violent lover?"

"Both. You know they went on sleeping together after they were divorced?"

It didn't surprise me. "People do."

"Why would anybody want to?"

"Gets to be a habit, I guess."

"It didn't sound like a habit, the way she wrote about it. According to her it got even better when they weren't married."

That didn't surprise me either.

"I don't think Rick beat her up or anything, but they liked to explore the outer limits, 'going over the edge' she called it. 'Rick took me over the edge last night,' she says. 'My bones dissolved in a purple mist.' Tell me something, Neil," Jamie asked, "do people really have experiences like that?"

"Yeah . . ."

Jamie sighed. "It's never been like that for me. I mean I always thought Tim and I were compatible and all, but it's just a physical release, I don't see colors or anything."

We were on squishy ground now so I moved on. "Did

you find what you were looking for in here?"

"I guess. I found out what she thought about Tim, anyway." Her hair had fallen back over her face, but this time she left it there. " 'Tim thinks he's in love with me.' " She mimicked Lonnie's voice perfectly, and why not? She'd known her her entire adult life and she'd probably read the passage over and over again. The point of journals apparently is to record your deepest, darkest thoughts, the thoughts you wouldn't share with anyone, until something happens to you and all those anyones read them. I've never kept one myself. Jamie shouldn't have read Lonnie's thoughts; Lonnie shouldn't have written them down or maybe even have thought them. " 'I love Tim, but I don't *love* him,' " Jamie continued in the same mimicking, vulnerable-but-charging-ahead-anyway voice. " 'He's just a friend, a good and dear friend, but I'm not in love with him, even if it weren't for Jamie, I wouldn't be in love with him. I couldn't love a man who writes me poetry. But how can I tell him that and not hurt him?' "

How could you tell Jamie that and not hurt *her?* Even the hair hanging over her face couldn't hide it. Thoughts are thoughts as long as you keep them inside your head. It's when they exit as words that they become bullets, projectiles with velocity and direction, zingers aimed at the target of the heart. It wasn't pleasant to know your man was in love with another woman. You wouldn't want him to get it on with her, but it wouldn't feel good to have him rejected by her either. In my book the odds of falling in love with someone who gives you no encouragement are poor. Flirting walks the thin line, that's what makes it interesting. Probably Lonnie had encouraged Tim. Like most people she'd done a lot of things she shouldn't have. And now she was dead. It didn't make me believe in karma; I was waiting to see about justice.

"It was just a fantasy of Tim's," I told Jamie. "After

twenty years everybody has fantasies, don't they?"

"I don't, Neil." Jamie started to cry. "I love Tim. I've never loved anybody but him. I wouldn't know how to fantasize, I wouldn't even know who to fantasize about."

Jamie's life had been concerned with perfecting the ordinary, not getting lost in purple mists. She got her satisfaction from doing things like cooking, sanding floors, shaping mud. If you ask me you have to like the ordinary to stay married. On the other hand, it takes a certain affection for the tacky to stay single, and what happens if you love the ugly? As the only man she'd known, Tim had probably been an archetype for all men, and compared to all men, he wasn't so bad. He'd never make any money, but not everybody cares about that. He was smart, he had integrity and a sense of humor. Better yet, to my way of thinking, he had dreams, but that's probably what had gotten them into trouble. "What are you going to do now?" I asked her.

"What can I do? What's out there for me without Tim? Affairs, living alone? That's fine for you, but it wouldn't work for me. I'm used to being a couple; it's all I know. We'll probably go on fighting until we get out of here. I'm hoping Ohio will help now."

"I hope so," I said. If you were into perfecting the ordinary, Ohio seemed like a good place for it. There were a couple of questions that remained to be asked. "I'm curious about something. Where did you get the money to fix up the house?"

"Borrowed it from Tim's brother. He made a killing when he sold his house in L.A."

"Did you find any more papers while you were here, say about Jorge Mondragon or the Ugly Building?"

"Yeah. They're in the back."

I opened the journal and found the papers folded up there like old maps. There were copies of paid hospital bills for Maria Mercedes Mondragon, over $100,000 worth, and a copy of a $200,000 second mortgage that Jorge Mondragon had recently paid off. Anybody could copy a paid-off mortgage note in the county court house. It probably wouldn't be that hard to get the hospital bills either. Lonnie could have stopped by, said she was Mondragon's secretary, that she'd lost the originals and didn't want her boss to know. Jorge Mondragon had had his reasons. He hadn't come cheap, but there seemed to be plenty of money where that $300,000 came from. The documents were a good motive for murder, only that murderer would have gotten them before killing Lonnie.

"I'm glad you called, Neil," Jamie said. "And I'm sorry I didn't call you first. I was just too embarrassed to admit that I'd come here and taken the journal. I'm not a secretive person and I'm glad to get it out. Also, this could be the proof needed to stop the Ugly Building, couldn't it?"

"Yes."

"I didn't know what to do with it."

"I do."

"Good. It was Lonnie's dream and I'd like to see it come true. It may be hard to believe, but I loved her, and I could understand why Tim did, too. She was so . . . so vulnerable, not like me. I'm competent."

"What's wrong with that?"

"Everybody depends on you. When you're vulnerable you can depend on them."

I believed in competence myself. "Listen, Jamie, there's another thing," I said. "The toilet seat was up. Did you do that or was someone else in here?"

"It was me. Lonnie always bitched about men leaving the seat up. I had to go to the bathroom and it was kind of a last-minute thought. I figured if I did that she wouldn't suspect *me* of taking the journal anyway."

"What does Tim know about all this?"

"He knows I took the car and went out in his shoes. He

knows I came here. I told him Lonnie wasn't home, that's all."

"There's one more thing. What did you do after you left here?" It was the last question that had to be asked of the woman who paid attention to the small things, the woman who smashed a hole in the wall when she wanted a window.

"Went to Dunkin' Donuts on Alcazar, had a cup of coffee, read the journal. Around three I went home."

"That's it? You never saw Lonnie again?"

"Well . . . actually I did. When I came out of Dunkin' Donuts I saw her turn down Miranda. She was alone in the car. I figured you had met someone at Club West and she was coming back here."

"She didn't come into the house if she did. Your footstep was on top in the morning." If Lonnie was the someone Rick picked up at Club West he must have brought her back to her car afterwards. She was on her way home alone, only something happened between the corner and 7½, some fatal decision was made, unless, of course, one of my best friends wasn't telling the truth.

"Maybe she did go out to the ruins alone," Jamie said.

"Maybe."

"What are you going to do with the journal, Neil?"

"Keep it for evidence," I said, although I wished I could throw it in the fire and watch it burn.

Jamie got in the Toyota and went home to Dolendo, part of a couple again. I did what the police should do at the start of an investigation—when they conduct an investigation: I went out to interview the neighbors.

My first stop was the garage-size hovel where the cute stray who called himself Dolby said he lived. There was a wall shedding stucco between 7½ and that building. It had an opening in it and I went through. Home was an adobe building that had begun the long slide back to dirt. The Harley-Davidson eagle had landed in the driveway. As I walked toward the door, I heard a woman yelling in one of those angry voices that's annoying during the day, terrifying when it wakes you at night. "Get out of here, you fucker," she screamed.

A man came outside and the door slammed behind him. He was a big guy with greasy black hair and a wide leather belt holding up his jeans. "Bitch," he said. "I paid her fifty bucks and she wasn't worth ten." He got on his motorcycle, gunned the engine and drove off.

I knocked on the door and the woman yanked it open. She had a pale, undeveloped, teenager's body—I could tell because she was wearing a miniskirt and strapless top that showed most of it. She had skinny arms and legs and skinny breasts, too, that barely held the top up. Women who don't have great bodies and advertise them anyway have a certain kind of nerve . . . or need. Under the mini she wore a black garter belt, the straps hanging down and holding up matching nylons. Pieces of skinny white thigh poked through. She had spiky blond hair. The body was childlike but the hair was dyed and the face was hard, pale and angry. She looked burned out, which isn't the same as looking old. I placed her in her early thirties, just old enough to have a teenage boy—if she'd started early. "Whatta you want?" she asked.

"I'm looking for Dolby," I said.

"Don't know him." She started to slam the door again.

"He's a cute blond kid who told me he lives here."

"Calls himself Dolby now?" She laughed, showing dark crevices between her teeth. "Christ, where'd he get that?"

"You two related?"

"You could say so, only to me he's Jim." And maybe that was why the blind old lady down the street didn't know who Dolby was either.

"I need to talk to him."

"That fucking kid in trouble again? Well you ain't likely to find him here. Me and this place are too messy for him." From what I could see over her shoulder, the house was messy all right, and a TV that was probably on twenty-four hours a day was blaring, too. "He's sixteen years old, got his own car, I can't do nothin' with him, never could, and he don't tell me nothin' never." She probably didn't tell him anything either, probably hadn't since she was his age and he stopped being a doll she could cuddle and coo to. "All he does when he's here is hang around and watch me. He oughta get himself his own place and soon, too. So, whatta you want him for?" She looked me over, and I hoped it wasn't a lawyer she was seeing. One of the reasons I like to go out in plain clothes is that nobody wants to tell anything to lawyers, even their own.

"I'm a friend of Lonnie Darmer's. Her place was broken into the night she died. I thought maybe Dolby—Jim—saw or heard something."

"When was that?"

"Saint Patrick's Day, weekend before last, the night it snowed."

"I don't remember for sure but that mighta been the weekend he slept all day. I never saw anyone sleep like him." She started to shut the door.

"Wait. Do you have any idea where I could find him?"

"Church?" She laughed and slammed the door in my face.

"Thanks," I said to the wood.

19

I got on the interstate and headed home. Out here where the sky is big and empty, you can watch the moon in all its phases. Tonight it was full; a hole in the sky, as some American Indians put it. The moon's light dimmed the stars but spotlighted the falcon clouds hanging on over Ortiz Mountain. The *peregrinos* beside the highway would have to do some fast walking—faster than springtime—if they were going to make it to Chimayo; tomorrow was Good Friday and they still had thirty miles to go. The flashlights they carried in their hands flickered like fireflies from a wetter place.

People who are in the business—cops, psychiatrists, emergency room nurses—say the full moon brings out aberrant behavior, but it wasn't creating any desire to howl, take mood-altering drugs or cross frontiers in me. What I wanted more than anything was to go home, lock myself in, dream of nothing. I thought about how I could get Dolby/Jim to tell all he'd seen without the aid of a police interrogation. At a time like this it's always tempting to fall back on the man in your life, and I had a flash of the Kid grabbing Dolby by the collar and shaking the truth loose. The Kid might even do it if I asked. I also saw me pointing my LadySmith and getting what I wanted. I'd fired a gun before, but I hadn't connected. Before any of this could take place, however, Dolby would have to be found.

As I attempted to climb La Bajada the legger balked and brought back thoughts of the ordinary, automobiles. The Kid expected the carburetor tomorrow and on Saturday intended to repair the Rabbit. Would it be worth it? I wondered. That car had been a piece of shit when I bought it and wasn't improving with age. It was three hundred for parts versus seven grand minimum for a new car. I've never had a new car, but it was an experience everyone should enjoy at least once in a lifetime. You could take good care of it, wash it every week, get the oil changed often, take it back to the dealer for all its service checks. A car like that would last years and be dependable. It wouldn't leave you stranded on the interstate or abandoned in Dolendo. It would be a loyal husband instead of a philandering lover. I thought about what I'd like to own, a black Saab turbo, maybe. They're big, heavy, solid—if something hits you you have half a chance, and they don't reveal too much about the driver either. But the Kid says they're a pain in the ass to work on. He likes Nissans and Toyotas. "They're good cars," he says. "And anybody can fix 'em."

The car that was passing me on the way up La Bajada wasn't a good car, it was a familiar-looking junker, a big gray American model that probably had a Garfield clawing at the window, although it was too dark out for me to see. Not a real low rider, it just naturally hung down almost far enough to scrape the highway. Still, it was passing me, which some people would consider an insult. There are people who shoot each other over things like this, but I took it calmly. What the heck, the legger wasn't really my car anyway, just a rental. I let the junker have its little victory, but I got pissed when it cut me off and slowed down so I was faced with the choice of creeping along behind it or passing. Creeping isn't an option I like to consider so I swung into the passing lane, stepped on the gas. "Come on, legger," I coaxed, "get yourself in motion." But just as I'd come to expect, it hesitated. Meanwhile the junker—which must have had a clutch and real gears—sped up, burned rubber and climbed over the top of La Bajada. The legger finally brought its attention back to the highway and went into passing mode, but it was too late, the junker was gone, another macho victory won.

Going down La Bajada was an improvement. Even the legger could speed downhill. I let it run, around the curves, down the dip, past the place where the pink cliffs rise from the arroyo. In the flat spot across the wash the rent-a-Ford headlights picked out a parked car poorly concealed by a couple of scrawny piñons. In the unlikely event a policeman was out patrolling I-25, I checked my speedometer—eighty—and slowed down. The waiting car pulled out behind me as I passed. There wasn't any blue light blinking from its roof or its dashboard either. It followed right along on my tail while I scrupulously obeyed the speed limit of sixty-five, and then, just to make sure I knew it was there, turned on the high beams. They weren't as bright as the A-bomb test sites where the scientists looked through their own skin and saw their bones, but bright enough to make me aware of the fragility of my skeletal structure. There wasn't anything I could do about it but keep on driving. To stop alongside the highway with someone behind me that I couldn't see didn't strike me as wise. LadySmiths were no good blind. We happened to be going up an incline and I couldn't go any faster. I leaned forward to avoid the blinding reflection from the rearview mirror. The move was probably visible to the person behind me, who was beginning to feel like a predator with me as the prey. We moved along like this testing nerves, but I guessed mine were stronger, because the junker picked up speed and passed me. I slowed down and let it go, watching the taillights move into the distance and disappear over an incline.

I'd been concentrating so hard on avoiding the high beams that I wasn't paying attention to where I was. An exit was coming up. There aren't many on this stretch of highway and few of them offer services. When you leave Albuquerque or Santa Fe you have to make sure you have enough gas to get to the other place, because there's nowhere to buy it in between. Experience indicated the junker would be waiting down the road to continue the chase, so I made a snap decision and took the exit. There were no highways leading to Santo Domingo Pueblo or Los Alamos here. I happened to have taken Budaghers, the exit to nowhere. I wasn't going far on this road, but ahead of me on the interstate lurked a full-moon crazy, so I decided to wait it out. The junker's driver would eventually get tired and move on, it wouldn't be coming back this way, anyhow. Maybe a caravan would come along that I could follow for protection, or maybe I would just stay here and wait for daylight and the pack of commuters. I had LadySmith, my personal protection, to get me through the night. I drove a couple of hundred feet to the Day-Glo fence that marked the end of the road and the beginning of desert, parked, turned off the lights and engine, put the car keys in my pocket, got the LadySmith out of the glove compartment, laid it on the seat and waited.

Waiting isn't my forte, but I'll do it when I have to. For once I wished I had a car phone. I've always suspected that people use them to dial the weather so they'll look good in traffic, but if I had one now I'd call 911, if there was a 911 in a place that doesn't exist. One way to get help would be to signal with my headlights, but who would get the message? There wasn't a house or building in the twenty-mile radius I could see. There weren't even any trees or piñons to hide me from the moon's light. I was at the top of an incline, visible to anyone who happened to look up from the highway, but no one was likely to. They'd be more interested in where they were going. My vantage, however, gave me a clear view of the interstate, two lanes heading north, two south, white lights coming, red going. The traffic was light in both directions. Although this wasn't a place I felt at home, it was better than confronting a moving vehicle. Cars are weapons, too, just as deadly as guns.

I waited. The rhythmic coming and going of lights—red, white; white, red—had a hypnotic effect, not enough to lull me into indifference or sleep, but enough to emphasize the break in the rhythm, whites where there ought to be reds, lights moving north in a southbound lane. Partners of light danced up the interstate, too regular, too evenly spaced, too fast, too bright to be fireflies or *peregrinos*. Someone was driving up I-25 the wrong way. A car heading south put its brake lights on and swerved to avoid a collision. The full-moon crazy stayed in the fast lane and kept on coming. When the vehicle got to the Budagher's exit, the driver flicked on the turn signal and pulled off. It was the gesture, maybe, of a compulsive person, but the driver left the signal on and it continued to flash as the car climbed the incline, drove to within about thirty feet of me and stopped. I turned my headlights on when the other car's went off. The driver got out and began to cross the no man's land between us in the glare of my high beams. He had draped a sleeping bag around his shoulders like a cape, the kind of cape that makes a boy a myth; its large, ominous shadow billowed and spread behind him. It was Dolby, the cute teenager, who had a junker of his own. I stepped out of the legger, pointed the LadySmith at him.

"Hey." He grinned. "Don't shoot."

"Drop the sleeping bag," I said.

"I might get cold."

"Drop it."

"Okay." He did it, a scrawny boy in a T-shirt and jeans who wore gardening gloves and had a bruise around his elbow.

"Walk over to my car, turn around, put your hands on the roof."

"You're the boss." He did as I said, put his hands against the roof and looked down. I walked up close and inspected his arm. Around his right elbow was a tattoo of a spiderweb with an insect in it. "Where'd you get the tattoo?"

"Guide Line. I heard you went there."

"Who told you that?"

"Checker."

"You were there, too?"

"Yeah. After you left I followed you up here. I saw you go to my mom's." She was his mother; it seemed like a stretch to call her a mom. "What'd you go see her for?"

I gripped the gun tight, took a deep breath, plunged in. "Because I want to know what happened the night Lonnie Darmer died. All of it."

He looked down at the ground, squirmed and poked the dirt with his shoe. "I don't remember. I was home, watching TV."

"I was in her house that night. I saw you leave with her." It wasn't the truth, but it might lead me there.

"You mighta seen somebody but it wasn't me."

"Who was it then?"

"Don't know, maybe my mom's boyfriend. Coulda been him."

"Yeah?" I tightened my grip on the gun.

He looked up from under his arms with a maybe I'll tell

you, maybe I won't expression, then he looked down and said, "Coulda been the other guy."

"What other guy?"

"The one she picked up on the street when she came home. That guy got thrown out of his house, see, in his T-shirt, no jacket or nothin', and Lonnie gave him her sleeping bag to keep him warm."

"What time was that?" I asked.

"Don't know, you'd have to ask him."

"Take a guess."

"Three, maybe."

"Did she take him to the ruins with her?"

"She mighta. She was kind of messed up and she wanted to hike into a cave and light a fire and stay there all night and watch the sun rise and then chant like the Indians did, you know. Don't know for sure, but I think he went. And after he got up there he'd want her to do somethin' to him, but she wouldn't want to, see. It was something his mother, no, his baby-sitter used to do to him. It was his baby-sitter, pull on him, you know, when he was little, sometimes she tied it to the drawer handle, shut it and pulled it open again. He liked it, but she laughed at him and he didn't like that. Your friend Lonnie, she wouldn't do nothin'." The words were pouring out of him like piss. Maybe he was bragging, maybe he was confessing. I was pointing a gun at him, but it didn't seem like fear was making him talk.

I went on asking—I had to. "Did he kill her because she wouldn't do it?"

"Don't know. You'd have to ask him. He didn't want to hurt her or nothin', he just wanted to do it his way. She wouldn't, but I don't think he killed her. I think he just put the bag over her face because she was crying—like a cat, see—and he hates that. She'd probably be alive today if she'd stopped crying. But he didn't kill her, he just put the bag over her face and she left."

I'd heard what I needed to. I should have shot him then, walked away and argued self-defense, if anybody cared. What was the point of wasting tax money keeping psychopathology like that alive? There was lots more of it around to study; science could proceed without his brain. But I didn't; I knew Bunny Darmer and everyone else would want their day in court. So, as if I was conducting a routine deposition, I continued the interrogation. "Where did she go?"

"Into the being of light. That's what Ci calls it."

"Does Ci know about this?"

"Only what he told her."

"Why didn't Lonnie struggle or fight back?"

"When she went out of the cave to look at the stars she left her coat. He took her pills, smashed them up and put them in the wine she was drinking so she got pretty messed up. She couldn't do nothin' once he put the cape on anyway, see. Nobody can do nothin' to him and nobody can laugh at him then, either, not his mother, not her boyfriends, nobody. After that he was sittin' on her and holding it to the ground right over her face so she couldn't move too much. She jerked around a little and when she was quiet he stood up and did it himself the way he wanted, but on the sleeping bag, see. He didn't leave her messy or nothin' and he put her coat over her to keep her warm. She looked like she was sleeping. Maybe she was. Yeah, I think she was sleeping when he left."

I only had one more question. "How did he get home?"

"He walked to the highway and hitched back in the morning. Slept all day when he got home. His mom couldn't figure out why he was sleepin' like that. He didn't hear her boyfriends comin' and goin' or nothin'. I know how he did it. You want me to show you?" He looked up from the ground, turned around, faced me.

"You stay where you are."

"It won't hurt." He dropped his hands, grinned a grin that had gone the fractional distance from cute to deadly and started walking toward me. "I'm just a kid, see, only sixteen years old. I couldn't hurt nobody."

Sixteen years old and invincible as Batman. Bullets would bounce off him, knives wouldn't pierce his skin, sixteen years old and a killer. He kept on coming, wanting me, maybe, to kill him. When you've got the disease, it doesn't matter who gets killed, but if that was what he wanted, I wouldn't do it. I wanted him to pay and pay for what he did. I wanted him to suffer. I wanted to blast away his killer's grin. I pointed the gun at his legs and pulled the trigger. There wasn't any explosion, kickback or speeding bullet, just a small, quiet click. I pulled and the trigger clicked again and again. His grin widened and fixed like a manic Garfield. I was stunned stupid by the gun's failure and he was on me, quicker and stronger than I would have expected. He grabbed my hand, twisted the gun out, pushed me to the ground, knelt down and straddled me. I struggled to get up, he slapped me back with his gloved hand and my head hit the ground so hard it bounced. The malice had spread from his heart to his fingers. He reached into his pocket, pulled out the missing bullets and began inserting them in the chambers one by one. "You shouldn't have left your window open when you parked your car at Checker's, see, you shouldn'ta done that. Anybody can get in through an open window. This wouldn't be happening now, if you hadn't done that."

One inch of window and my death would be all my fault, because with killers like him it's always what *you* did that caused it. They may feel sorry—briefly—later, but it's your fault. You left your windows open or you didn't; you wore high-heel shoes, you wore Keds. They kill you if you wear a skirt, or Levi's. They kill you when you cry, when you don't. They kill you because you're a twenty-year-old who fucks around, because you're an eighty-year-old virgin. They kill you if you're a cat, or a woman, because they have the killing disease, because you get in the way. Killers kill whether you plead, yield or fight back, but at least if you fight back you have a chance to escape.

He kept the gun pointed at me, and I didn't move. I waited for my head to stop throbbing and my vision to clear. He got off me and walked over to the legger, dragging a shadow that was ten feet long until he turned the headlights off. The moon's light made him underbelly pale, but at least it brought him back to human size. I slid my hand in my pocket, felt the car keys there. He picked up the sleeping bag, draped it over his shoulders like the empowering cape he thought it was and began walking back holding the gun on me all the while, but shooting wasn't his modus operandi, the one that had memories and meaning for him. His MO was the ritualized act of a serial killer, one that was going to turn me into bones beside the highway. Still, hot fear climbed my throat like vomit when he knelt over me and put the gun against my neck.

"You want to pull it?" He grinned.

"Get off of me, you little shit."

"Hey," he said. "You shouldn't talk like that, not to me, see."

He had to put the gun somewhere so his hands were free to do their killer work. He stuck it into the waistband of his jeans and then, kneeling on me with his knees pressing my shoulders into the ground, he lifted the cape. This can't be happening, I thought. It's a dream. Any minute now I'll wake up in my bedroom and he'll be gone. He pulled it over his head and for a long moment he was invincible and we were both in darkness. Then he bunched it up and pressed it over me and me alone, the cape of smothering oblivion. "Get off of me," I tried to scream, but the words got squashed in my throat. I didn't give a shit about beings of light or what was on the other side. I was looking at death, black death with every bit of the responsibility, and life was what I wanted, air, light and life. Lonnie, Lonnie, Lonnie, I thought, why didn't you fight back? His knees pinned my arms to the ground, but my legs were free. I jerked them up, kicked and bucked. There was no technique or plan to it, just fear, adrenaline and a fierce desire to live. I put everything I had into motion. He was in his killing trance, not expecting resistance. I couldn't reach his body with my kicks but I did throw him off balance. As he put his left hand on the ground to steady himself, my right arm came loose. I reached into my pocket, clutched the car keys in my fist and stabbed at him. He put his hand up to stop me and the keys stabbed his palm. I stabbed again and gouged his face. As he jerked away from me, he dropped the sleeping bag and the gun fell out of his waistband. I lunged at him. He smacked my hand hard, the keys flew out onto the ground and he grabbed them. Then he went for the gun, but I had gotten there first. He knelt on top of the sleeping bag, keys in hand, and stared at me with a dazed comprehension that maybe he, Dolby and Jim were one, that this wasn't a boy's game, that I wasn't his mother, that the gun was in my possession now. He jumped up and began to run. I fired at him and hit his arm, which he clutched to his side. I pulled the trigger and grazed his leg, but he continued running crookedly toward his car. I shot the car, blew a front tire. He darted over the incline, heading for the interstate.

I saved my bullets in case he came back. When I couldn't see him anymore I crawled over, sat down and leaned against my car. My head was throbbing. I couldn't move. I couldn't do anything but sit there, try to calm the trembling gun and listen to cars pass like waves on the interstate. After a while a flashlight came over the rise. Whoever was holding it could see me a lot clearer than I could see them, but I was ready to fire.

"She'll shoot you, Tomás, if you don't turn that thing off."

The flashlight went out. "Don't shoot," Tomás said. "We're *peregrinos* on our way to Chimayo. We won't hurt you."

I could see by the moonlight that they were two dumpy guys with a day pack and a water jug. They'd probably been hiking for twenty miles and felt every bit of it.

"We crossed over the highway and were waiting down there for Tomás's wife, when we heard the gunshots," the other guy said. "Then we saw the boy running away."

"That boy tried to kill me."

"Are you all right?"

"I think so."

Tomás looked at the ground. In the moonlight you could see clearly the trail of blood. "He won't get far like that. Why was he trying to kill you?"

"I'm a woman. I got in his way."

"The world is a bad place." Tomás shook his head. "Every year we go to Chimayo to say a prayer that it will get better."

Somebody had to. My head had stopped pounding enough so I could think about the next steps, getting to the cops, getting home. "He took the keys to my car."

"My wife is coming to pick us up soon. We can take you home or anywhere else you want."

"How about Santa Fe?"

"No problem."

We walked down to I-25, sat on the ground and waited. I wasn't in any shape to walk further and neither were they. I kept the gun in my hand and brought the sleeping bag with me. It would have been better not to disturb the crime scene, but it was evidence and the killer might come back for it. "We always go to Chimayo to say prayers," said Tomás's friend, whose name I never did learn. "First it was for my brother who was killed in Vietnam, but every year there's somebody."

Tomás's wife arrived eventually in an old Ford. She kept staring over the top of her glasses like she didn't know what to make of me and my gun. Although we watched carefully beside the highway while we drove to Santa Fe, we didn't see Dolby or Jim. Railback wasn't on duty, but the policeman who was believed my story. No doubt I looked battered enough to be convincing, or maybe Tomás, his wife and friend gave me credibility. We went back to the crime scene and found too much evidence for anybody to screw up.

20

There are places on the high road to Taos where you think your destiny must be the cumulonimbus. Chimayo is in a narrow valley off that road, a sacred place and a kind of paradise, a paradise with poverty. The Adobe of God's walls are three feet thick and it hunkers down at the center of the valley near a mountain stream. Fruit trees bloom there in springtime. In the meadow across the stream, horses and junked cars graze. There's a cross in the yard that a penitent carried on his back from Santa Fe, thirty miles away. Inside the sanctuary you can dig into the floor and take away some healing earth. Many leave their crutches behind with pictures commemorating the healing.

On Good Friday the Santuario is full of penitents, celebrants and tourists. Railback found Dolby among the crowd with a wounded arm and leg and bloody marks that I'd gouged on his face and palms. He held his palms up and grinned when they arrested him. "Hey, that guy, he's sorry," Dolby said. It was the closest they ever got to a confession out of him. He wasn't so eager to talk in a police station or a courtroom. Dennis Quinlan, however, was a hardworking and thorough prosecutor. He had me for a witness and the sleeping bag with Dolby's semen stains and Lonnie's and my saliva.

Marci Coyle was convicted of bribing a public official and Jorge Mondragon of accepting. They both paid large fines but neither spent time in jail. Rick admitted, to me anyway, that Lonnie had found him at Club West and they had had sex at his place the night she died. He had inflicted the rough, consensual bruises—body and soul. In an angry moment Marci Coyle admitted to Rick that she had stayed in Santa Fe to check up on him and had seen him and Lonnie leave Club West together. He told her that he'd talked to Lonnie and that was all they'd done. Apparently Marci chose to believe it; she stayed with him anyway. Maybe she thought with Lonnie dead she had nothing more to worry about. Tim and Jamie Malone went to Ohio, a couple again, and they seemed to like the Midwest. Tim said that everyone of Celtic origin should have the opportunity to dream life in a green-gray womb. The Ugly Building did not get built, but there was an empty lot on Paloma and it wouldn't stay empty forever. A shopping mall was waiting in the wings and, if that didn't get approved, a hotel was right behind it.

Dolby's mother went to Texas after he was arrested and never came back. Ci paid for his defense. "Lonnie's gone now," she said, "we have to do what we can to create better conditions for Dolby in the next incarnation." He was tried as an adult, but he acted like a boy, joking all the while and smiling for the cameras.

Bunny Darmer sat in the courtroom for the entire trial and never took her eyes off Dolby/Jim. "How could he do it?" she asked me at one point. "How could that young boy kill my daughter?"

I, who knew better than anyone, had to answer, "I don't know." It's a crime of subjugation and humiliation, some people say, not sex, but it was a long time before I wanted to have sex again.

Every prosecutor knows it's difficult to convict a good-looking defendant and that much harder when the defendant is young. Dennis Quinlan had the facts, me and Lonnie on his side. He presented a good case, I thought, and gave an impassioned summation. "He was an evil seed who wanted to prove that he was a man," Dennis said. "He has the appearance of a boy but don't let that fool you, he has the power of a man to harm and destroy. He hates women and wants to crush them. He terrorized Neil Hamel. He witnessed and caused the last moments of horror in Lonnie Darmer's short life."

When it was over Dolby was convicted of second-degree murder and sentenced to fifteen years to be served at the Santa Fe state pen. When he graduated from that place he'd have an advanced degree in sex abuse and a Ph.D. in killing. I began looking at fifteen years—or less—down the road. Bunny Darmer went home to Roswell, got into her bathrobe and began serving her life sentence.

When spring turned to summer it got hot: 102, 103, 104. A closed car was a death trap. The air became your enemy. It got hot enough to crank up the air conditioner and crawl under a blanket, but I didn't do it. Anything on top of me—even a sheet—weighed far too much. Through the summer nights I sweated, tossed, and barely breathed. I didn't open the window either because he was out there. Every night before I went to sleep (if you could call it that) I bolted the door, closed the window, and latched it tight.

But he got in anyway, a Superboy who slips through windows and walls. "You shouldn'ta done that," he said. "This wouldn't be happening now if you hadn'ta done that." It was a ritualized and practiced act. His cape swung from his shoulders. He lifted it, grinned, pressed smothering oblivion over my face. I couldn't breathe; lights were spinning in the void. "No, no, no!" I screamed until I woke up, found myself alone in bed shaking and drenched with sweat. Any counselor will tell you that women shouldn't sleep alone after experiences like I'd had. It takes more than locks to keep the killers away.

A light went on in the living room. "Who's there?" I cried.

"It's me, Chiquita. It was too hot in the bedroom. I came out here and opened the window." The Kid came in, sat down on the bed. "You were having that dream?"

"Yeah. He's killing me over and over again."

"Think about what they will do to him in prison."

I did, but it didn't help. The Kid was beside me and that did. His skin felt cool to the touch. That's about all we'd been doing this summer—touching. Sex was a distant stranger, but the Kid had been patient. Night after night he'd slept out there.

"Chiquita, maybe I could open the window a little and sleep in your bed tonight?"

"Okay," I said.

It had rained earlier and cooled off. Once the window was open to the night air the Kid rolled over and went right to sleep. He always does.

I curled up behind him and gave his skinny shoulder a kiss.

"Thanks, Kid," I said.